SANE NEW WORLD
Replacing Values

Acknowledgements

Many people have helped me with this project. I would like to give particular thanks to Lyn Corson who began as copy editor, became interested in the ideas and organised the production of the book. I would also like to thank my friends at Millbank Books — Diana Walsh, Chris Walsh and Joan Ward — who guided the book through its early stages.

I gave the book to specialists to comment on each chapter. They were as follows:

Chapter One and Two: Bob Wharton, Management Consultant
Chapter Three: David Harrison of City University
Chapter Four: Dr Marion Newman, a General Practitioner, and Mrs Wendy Savage consultant obstetrician at the London Hospital.
Chapter Five: Dr Roger Matthews — Course Leader of the M.A. in Criminology, Middlesex Polytechnic.
Chapter Six: Dr Geoff Dench, Head of School of Sociology Middlesex Polytechnic

Thanks also to Rab MacWilliam, Ron Cunnington, Jane Stott, Tony Porter, Angela Mansi, Sam Beadle, Alan Honorof and Professor John Stancer.

SANE NEW WORLD
Replacing Values

Colin Francome

First published in 1990 by Carla Publications

Carla Publications
Centre for Community Studies
Queensway
Enfield
Middlesex EN3 4SF
England

ISBN 0 904804 97 6

Phototypesetting by The Works, Exeter, Devon, EX4 3LS, England. Printed and bound in Great Britain by Dotesios Printers Ltd, Trowbridge, Wilts.

This book is dedicated to my son, Russell,
who will be sixteen in the year 2000

Contents

SANE NEW WORLD
Replacing Values

Chapter 1

Introduction

The increase in concern about the environment has grown to an extent unimaginable only a few years ago. The response of the major political parties has been in part to play down the problem and in part to try and dress up one or two of their own policies.

What this book is calling for however, is not simply for greater concern with environmental issues but rather for far more radical changes throughout the whole of social life. The central theme of the book is that we should be moving beyond the old goals of wealth and property. We have the potential to move towards a different kind of lifestyle where people's lives are far more interesting, where they can develop their talents without society's limitation to prescribed roles, where crime is greatly diminished, where health care is available for all and treatment is carried out for the benefit of people and not the pursuit of profit. We need to look beyond old ideologies of communism and capitalism and seek out a caring world where people can live in harmony.

One of the central themes of the book is double alienation. The populations of the rich countries have an education system geared, in many respects, towards producing a workforce to increase wealth rather than an education that develops their personality. So people in general do not reach their full potential in terms of their creativity. Furthermore they are alienated from the realities of life experienced by people in poor countries. The famines which are documented on television do, of course, affect people and many make great voluntary contributions towards helping the poor. However, the scale of the effort is by no means equal to the task in hand.

In order to appreciate the scale of the problem let us consider some facts.

PRESENT FAILURES

When asked if she had eaten, the eight year-old Brazilian girl, the eldest of five, replied:

> 'Yes miss, yesterday Mummy made little cakes from wet newspapers'. Her parents had gone foraging in the garbage heaps and she continued: 'Mummy takes a sheet of newspaper, makes it into a ball and soaks it in water and when it's nice and soft kneads it into little cakes. We eat them, drink some water and feel nice and full inside'.

The Chicago Tribune opened 1988 with a story about a nine year-old mentally retarded boy, Keko Bullock and his fifty-two year-old father. The report noted that they did not have any lights and that his father 'braces for the winter with heavy coats and quilts as he struggles to make ends meet'. The father said that he never thought anyone went through what he was suffering, and the newspaper reported that while he spoke, his breath made puffs of vapour as candles cast dancing shadows on the wall of his apartment. Their troubles stemmed from the fact that when the father was laid off from his job he could no longer afford child care and had to go on state aid. His rent was more than his public aid check and his electricity was cut off when he became $2,517 in arrears.

These two children are being brought up in unnecessary poverty. They illustrate the fact that we need to change the values and economic structure of the world.

There are many other examples of unnecessary suffering. In this book we will look at some of them, their causes and make suggestions as to what *you* can do to change things. Here are some further facts to be considered.

★ We will close the twentieth century with four times the number of people as we had at the beginning. Most of the population growth is occurring in countries where malnutrition is most serious. One study has estimated that more than 1.1 billion people live in areas of the developing world where the population has already exceeded the carrying capacity of the land.

★ The World Bank has estimated that there are between 340 million and 730 million people in developing countries (excluding China) who do not have sufficient income to avoid serious health risks and prevent stunted mental and physical growth in children.

★ This a world in which some rich countries have so much food that they do not know what to do with it, yet children of the poor very often go to bed cold and hungry. The United States had almost twice the daily calorie supply per head as Bangladesh in 1985.

★ The United Nations Children's Fund reports that somewhere in the world a young child dies every 2 seconds, which is more than 40,000 children each day. It has developed a fourfold plan which when used fully, will reduce the deaths by half. The plan is growth monitoring, breast feeding, techniques to get children to retain water, and immunisation. The cost of these things is low — what is needed is the will.

★ People in poor countries are having far more children than they want. A 1987 survey of developing countries showed less than one in five had good access to birth control. If everyone who wanted family planning could get it, the birth rate in poor countries would drop by more than a third. In 1987 the women had an average of over six children each in Iran, Zaire, Zimbabwe, Pakistan, Nigeria, and Ethiopia. They had an average of over seven children in Zambia, Tanzania, Jordan and Afghanistan. In Kenya the average woman had eight children.

★ There is evidence that resources necessary for food production in many regions are under great stress and there are growing problems of deforestation, soil degradation and desertification. Tropical forests have been reduced by 38% in Latin America and 23% in Africa in a little over a quarter of a century.

★ The world military expenditure budget exceeds £500 billion a year, while the cost of immunising every child in the world against killer childhood diseases would be about £350 million a year — less than the world spends on the military every six hours today. We spend the same amount every hour on the military as was spent over 20 years ago to eradicate the killer disease, smallpox.

★ The African famine of 1984 led to citizens of the world wondering what they could do to help. Yet British groups made five visits to the general area, not to help but to try to sell weapons. The lack of real help was evident from the fact that in 1985, for every pound given to Africa to help famine relief, the West reclaimed two pounds in debt payments.

★ Over twenty-five years ago, President Kennedy said that the United States had the ability to destroy the Soviet Union twice over while the Soviet Union could only destroy the United States once. The Soviet leader Kruschev agreed but joked that he was not complaining: 'We're satisfied to be able to finish off the US first time round. Once is quite enough. What good does it do to

9

annihilate a country twice'. Since that time arms expenditure has grown so that each country could now destroy the whole world many times over.

★ World health care is abysmal. In rich countries like the United States, people have more than twice as many operations as are necessary for good health, due in part to the profits that can be made from them. I discuss this in more detail in Chapter Four. Even in Britain there has been an increase in unnecessary surgery as doctors carry out operations not because they are medically justified but rather to protect themselves in case things go wrong. This is particularly true of Caesarean sections. In poor countries medical care is not readily available to those in need and the average length of life is much shorter than it should be. For every 100,000 women having babies, 3,000 will die in Bangladesh compared to around ten in the United States and less than 2 in Norway.

★ The rich countries have been taken over by consumerism. They are creating so much waste that getting rid of rubbish is an increasing problem. Tokyo is expected to run out of space for waste before the end of the century, and in the United States more than half the states will use up most of their landfill sites before the year 2,000.

★ At the start of 1990 one in five US children were living in poverty. The crime rates in rich countries like Britain and America have more than doubled over the last ten years and their governments have still not realised that this rise is due to policies which promote greed and create poverty. Their only real response has been the suggestion to increase punishment. There is another alternative. In particular we need a change in society's values away from the amassing of wealth and ownership and towards a society where people want to develop their abilities and help others to improve their lives.

★ In rich countries one of the greatest failures is that of education. The education system in most of the developed world is geared to produce people for the workforce. It squeezes the originality from people on the grounds that it is necessary for the country to be competitive. The recent changes in Britain are accentuating this trend.

GROUNDS FOR OPTIMISM

Despite the fact that social and economic policies have been largely
misdirected there are some bright spots. Several countries have

reduced their birth rates to more manageable levels. For example, in Singapore the number of babies fell from over six per woman in 1960 to less than two in 1987, although some have criticised the fact that the country has different policies according to ethnic groups and actually encourages high fertility amongst ethnic Chinese. Over the same period Mexico reduced its births from 7.2 to 4.0, in Tunisia it was reduced from 7.3 to 4.5, and India reduced its family size from 6.2 to 4.3. Cuba and Costa Rica have also been successful in their family planning programmes so there are signs of progress.

During the period 1976-1980 food production in developing countries increased by 3.1% a year while the population only increased by 2.4% a year. This meant the number of calories per head increased from 2,340 to 2,630 across the decades 1961-1981. In part due to their reduction in population increase, China and India became self sufficient in grain/cereal production.

In 1985, although there was a disastrous food crisis in Ethiopia, 12 African countries were able to produce food surpluses totalling nearly three and a half million tons.

In the rich countries there are signs that they are at last beginning to move towards more sensible policies. The changes in Eastern Europe will lead to great possibilities in the reduction of arms expenditure and people will be increasingly able to spend their resources fighting poverty, rather than concentrating on fighting each other. Indeed an article in *Soviet Weekly* (6 Aug. 1989) I bought in Moscow made this very point and, in addition, called for aid to be freed from ideological restraints. In the US Michael Deland, who chairs President Bush's Council on Environmental Quality, said that both Americans and Russians must cleanse their hands and make fundamental changes in their lifestyle (*New York Times* 3rd Sept. 1989). This concern with the environment being shown by the European countries is a sign that at last the pressure from both the ordinary population and scientists is beginning to be heeded.

There is a long way to go and great problems to be solved, but there are indications that we are beginning to move in the right direction.

SOLUTIONS ON OFFER

In this section I want to briefly consider the solutions on offer, and in particular the failure of the dominant political groups, before outlining the proposals of this book.

MRS THATCHER AND MR BUSH — THE MARXISTS

One of the great mistakes of Western civilisation is to misunderstand what Marxism is all about. It is important to have some understanding of his appeal if any insight into the past of the countries of Eastern and Central Europe and China is going to be gained.

Mr Bush in his inaugural address as President in January 1989 said 'A new breeze is blowing and a world refreshed by freedom seems reborn'. Mrs Thatcher too has stressed the importance of freedom and in this concern they are stressing the central point of Marxism.

One of the strange facts is that they, and many other major political leaders in Britain and the United States, often think that they are opposed to Marxism. On 10 April 1989, as she approached ten years in power, Mrs Thatcher was quoted in The Independent as saying 'Marxism is a superficial creed, while ours is deeply grounded in religion and a faith in human nature'. She continued to state that socialism in general was not about human beings, but about economic plans and people having to conform to them, not about government serving the fundamental dignity and freedom of the individual.

This comment reveals how little Mrs Thatcher knows about Marxism. In fact the fundamental idea of Marxism is that individuals should be free to develop their personality and social relationships. Marx believed that the social conditions of the nineteenth century were preventing people from reaching their full potential. Anyone who has read through the reports of children working overlong hours down the mines, or in industry, would be hard put not to agree with him on this point.

Many among the right-wing think that Marxism is about promoting equality at the expense of the individual. However, he was more concerned that countries should develop the kind of societies where people's material wants would be catered for leaving them free to spend their time productively.

A further area of life where modern right-wing thinkers have similarity with Marx is on the question of government interference. Marx believed in the withering away of the state and that people should have control of their own lives. This is in sympathy with the right-winger's belief that there should be minimum state intervention. On this theme on 31 May 1989, President Bush called upon the Soviet Union to pull down the Berlin Wall. This is just the kind of action that would have appealed to Marx who would have been appalled that such restrictions on people's freedom could be imposed.

A further important similarity is that Marx, in common with right-wing politicians, realised the power of the media. Marx stated in the German Ideology that the ideas of the ruling class were the ruling ideas. Those in charge of society can influence the presentation of information in a favourable light. Right-wing politicians too realise this. Margaret Thatcher in particular has noted that the British newspapers are owned by businessmen sympathetic to her view. When she celebrated her tenth anniversary as Prime Minister, on the top table with her was one commoner, a Mr Rupert Murdoch. Faced with a more independent BBC, she has done what she could to have her allies appointed to positions of power.

Many politicians have tried to link Marxism with state control and lack of freedom as evidenced by restrictions on the movements of citizens from some countries. However, the strong state controls of some nominally Marxist countries are in direct opposition to views expressed in Marx's writing.

An important difference in belief between right-wingers and Marx is in their perspective on the role of capitalism. Marx believed that capitalism would produce such great wealth that eventually people would not have to work hard at boring jobs. They would live interesting lives with more free time for leisure and recreation activities. Right-wing politicians tend to view the world as producing ever increasing wealth. So this is a major difference in perspective.

While Marx's analysis was wanting in many areas, for example his belief that nationalism would disappear and that there would be worldwide revolution, nevertheless his view that capitalism could liberate people from arduous labour is an important point.

THE FAILURE OF RIGHT-WING IDEALS

The right-wing has been in power in both Britain and the White House for the whole of the 1980's. In the United States, however, right-wing influence has been diluted by the fact that although it has had a Republican President, the Congress has been Democrat. In Britain the lack of separation of powers has meant that the country has undergone a great experiment, as the Government has tried to create an enterprise culture. The Thatcher administration came in just as Britain's North Sea oil was coming on-stream. The extra money could have been used to improve the environment, to help the poor both in Britain and the rest of the world and to put the country on a sound financial basis. However, by the end of the decade both Britain and the United States were nations with serious balance of payments deficits. They had also cut back on their help to the poorer nations. Britain was well below international targets and the United States had, for example, pulled out of helping International Planned Parenthood Federation set up to help people choose the size of their family.

In addition both countries had great problems of poverty at home, with the streets of London increasingly following those of New York. Many of those who had been turned out of mental hospitals were sleeping on the streets. At the beginning of 1989 it was estimated that there were 60,000 teenagers in London alone without a fixed address. The prisons in both countries are bulging at the seams with Britain having more inmates per head of population than any other country in the European Community. According to the National Schizophrenia Fellowship many of the mentally ill are now wrongfully in prison. In the United States the tough policies towards criminals have not attacked the root cause of crime and people are still at great risk of being robbed or attacked.

As far as health care is concerned, in both countries it is much worse than comparable European societies. So the question must be asked: what has gone wrong?

A central reason for the problems lies in the interpretation of right-wing doctrine. This dates back to the ideas of Adam Smith in the *Wealth of Nations* originally published in 1776. An essential element in Smith's work was a belief in pursuit of self interest. In his view the greatest good of the community was served by people following their own interests — by pursuing their selfish ends they could promote those of the society more effectively than by acting altruistically. So in the right-wing view, a rational selfishness was the best course to follow. Smith argued it was not through the benevolence of the butcher, the brewer, or the baker, that people were fed, but due to their regard for their own interest. He believed that the best kind of society was one where altruistic relationships were limited to the immediate family. Other relationships should be carried out on the basis of beneficial exchange. Adam Smith also took the view that the role of government should be very limited.

Economists criticise this general theme that the pursuit of self interest will serve the general good on four main grounds. Firstly that it will generally not be true when there is monopoly power. In such conditions the suppliers can introduce built-in obsolescence more easily as will be discussed in Chapter Two. Secondly, external costs may be borne by others, not the decision maker. Pollution is a good example of this. For example the emissions of carbon dioxide leading to the greenhouse effect will not be prevented unless governments take action. In other areas too such as noise pollution, petrol fumes and radioactive emissions, the 'guiding hand of the market' can lead to disaster.

A third point is that there may be external benefits. It is for this reason that countries usually give large subsidies to public transport systems. Right-wing governments have often ignored the external benefits of public expenditure and this has often led to 'private affluence and public squalor'. The lack of public expenditure, and in particular the central control of the health service, is one of the reasons that health in the United States is much worse than comparable European countries.

Finally, if income distribution is not optimal this leads to an over-production of luxury goods and an under-production of the basic commodities. Many examples of this will be given in this book but it is clear that on a world level there needs to be a widespread change in production. There are other points critical of the Right I would like to add. By placing so much emphasis on money, governments are spreading false values. There is a role for people to protect their own interests and those of their family. However, it is also the case that the well-being of everyone in society is the joint responsibility of all. Additionally, in order to create the kind of emphasis on economic activity that the Right seeks, it is necessary to create insecurity. There must always be the possibility of failure. So such things as a social security service protecting people 'from the cradle to grave' are an anathema to the right-wing.

One of the most heartening events in 1988 was that both President Bush and Mrs Thatcher moved away from the extreme right-wing position and even began to take an interest in green issues. Although this might be seen as simple electioneering, however, it is now evident that the extreme right-wing experiment has run its course.

THE FAILURE OF THE LEFT

The Left in the United States has been operating in an environment much to the right of that in Britain and most of the developed world. The problem of 'private affluence and public squalor', a much used phrase in Galbraith's best known work *The Affluent Society,* is a feature of American society. Galbraith suggested that the general view in the United States is that while private production is important, public services are a burden. He suggested this attitude led to contradictions. So vacuum cleaners to provide clean houses are welcome while street cleaners are an unfortunate expense. Galbraith was one of the foremost advocates of public spending as a means of improving society.

In recent years there has been, in the United States, a debate between those characterised as liberals, who support high taxes and high public spending, and those arguing the case for low taxes so freeing the economy to go in whatever direction the market sends it. This has escalated to a point where, in his successful campaign for the presidency, George Bush made a pledge that he would not raise taxes. *The Guardian* (8th November 1988) set out the choice for the American people as follows:

THE CHOICE FOR AMERICA

BUSH	DUKAKIS
ECONOMY	
Proposed a flexible freeze on government spending and has	Decrying American position as number one debtor nation, he

BUSH	DUKAKIS
pledged not to levy new taxes. Does not specify what programmes might be frozen to reduce the federal deficit.	says 'tough choices' will have to be made; taxes would be raised only as a last resort.

DEFENSE

Hawkish on defense spending and is committed to star wars and 'modernising' NATO.	Toughening up his position after Republican attacks. He stresses the need to augment conventional force capabilities.

SOVIET UNION

Welcomes Gorbachev's reform programmes but is urging caution. Stressing his foreign policy experience, he has offered an early summit.	Would press Moscow to halt the development of new weapons systems, to co-operate on terrorism and improve its human rights and emigration record.

CENTRAL AMERICA

Takes a hardline stance, favouring a resumption of military aid to the Contras and pledging to combat the 'communist threat' in a number of countries.	Opposed to renewed aid to Nicaraguan rebels. Declaring a war on poverty, he proposes a hemispheric co-operation conference.

ENVIRONMENT

Backs further nuclear power plant construction; does not specify how to deal with existing crumbling reactors. A green convert, he now opposes offshore drilling.	Would expand the Environmental Protection Agency, which would have a seat in cabinet. Tough position on air, water pollution, acid rain and opposes radioactive waste.

DRUGS

Would appoint Quayle to head task force to combat drug threat, stressing rehabilitation, education and interdiction. He pledges to impose the death penalty on trafficker king pins.	Emphasising the menace 'that is poisoning our kids and our neighborhoods'. He would cut off aid to producing countries refusing to co-operate. Would beef up Coast Guard.

GUN CONTROL

Opposes federal gun registration or the licensing of gun owners.	Would outlaw the easily concealed Saturday night specials

'Should free men and women have right to own a gun to protect their home?' I say 'yes'. frequently used in crimes and generally favours tougher gun controls.

What is clear from this list is that there is no recognition of the fact that the United States needs to make fundamental changes to its policies in order that it can approach the quality of life enjoyed in other countries. The voters in the US did not have an opportunity to vote for a proper integrated health service, a transfer of resources from armaments to development, nor for the social and economic changes in attitude needed to reduce the crime wave.

One reason why these choices were not available is that the debate has not yet reached this level in the general population. One of the major tactical errors of the Left has been its failure to demonstrate the links between more left-wing policies and freedom. The Right have been able to present themselves as the supporters of freedom, in contrast to the Left who favour equality, which the Right consider as a levelling down. What the Left needs to stress is that, unless people have good social conditions, they cannot be free. Children raised in poverty without adequate diets are not free. Without adequate food they do not even reach their potential intelligence level. Economics and industry are there to serve the people and provide their basic needs. The goal in life should not be to store up wealth and own more and more. The aim should be to provide as much freedom as possible to allow people to live out their lives in the best way possible.

The British Left has failed to reach office since 1979, largely due to its internal squabbles. One of the sad things is that the debate has been on the wrong issues. It has not been considering the important issues of where society is going, how to create a sense of community, how to do away with the pre-eminence of economic factors or similar issues. It has been fighting over whether there should be total nationalisation of the whole of industry. Thus it has been fighting on a platform which is not really relevant to the important change of direction that is needed.

During the 1970's when I was actively involved in local politics, it was very clear to me that the Labour Party had a problem. The local activists were very much more to the left politically than both the Members of Parliament and the population of the country. What the party clearly needed to do was introduce 'one person, one vote' and aim for policies more relevant to the modern age. In fact, what it did was to extend the power from the Members of Parliament to the activists. This led to the damaging split, with some on the right of the party deserting to the Social Democrats and oblivion, and the party has been virtually unelectable for a long period.

It now has a set of policies more in tune with the feelings of the electorate. A Labour government would restore some of the benefits that have been taken away leading to poverty traps and would be more sympathetic to helping public transport with the resultant health benefits. It is also becoming more concerned with the environment. However, it still supports economic growth which is something that needs serious reassessment. In addition, it has yet to seriously address the fact that we do need fundamental changes in society so that the social order does not prevent people living their lives to the full.

THE GREEN VIEW

One of the most important books in terms of changing ideas was Schumacher's *Small is Beautiful* first published in 1973. It had a number of themes. One was that the goals of society, as put forward by the major industrial powers, were wrong. Schumacher opposed the idea that the levels of consumption enjoyed by the United States could be sustained on a worldwide basis. He pointed out that there is simply not enough energy in the world for every country to use in the same way.

He attacked the idea of ever expanding wants and drew attention to the fact that John Maynard Keynes, probably the most influential economist this century, had said that one day the time would come when avarice and usury would not be people's Gods but that people would once more value ends above means and would prefer the good to the useful. Schumacher concurred with this view and suggested that economically, our 'wrong' living consists primarily in systematically cultivating greed and envy and thus building up a vast array of unwarrantable needs.

One of his most important suggestions was that Third World countries should not follow the rich countries in seeking labour saving devices — instead they should use technology which employed their abundant labour force.

The phrase 'small is beautiful' was developed as a suggestion that many small countries and companies have been very successful and furthermore, large companies have often been more successful if they have been able to create the climate or feeling that they are part of a federation of quasi firms.

Jonathan Porritt's book *Seeing Green* sets out a number of problems which he sees as facing the world. He lays stress both on the problems of over-population and the fact that topsoil is being threatened by modern farming methods. He quotes a UN Food and Agriculture Organisation report of 1980 which stated that between 13 and 17 million acres of cropland were lost every year — exactly at the time when production will need to double in order to feed the world's increased population. He notes future problems with food production and in particular the dangers of over-fishing. With the disappearing rain-forests he identifies the problems of climate that might result from this.

On resources he follows Schumacher in being concerned with the general lack of oil reserves, pointing out that if everyone in the world consumed oil at the rate of the United States then supplies would be exhausted in fifteen years. He suggests that rich countries should be placing their emphasis on developing ways of obtaining energy from renewable resources such as wave and wind power.

He focuses on a number of other issues — the problems of the greenhouse effect, and the effect of pollution such as acid rain. He notes that the US Environmental Protection Agency estimates acid rain damage to buildings in the US at more than $2 billion each year. He sees the capitalist societies of the West and the 'Communist' countries of the East as producing similar problems commenting *a filthy smoke-stack is still a filthy smokestack whether it is owned by the state or a private corporation'*.

He proposes a number of factors that contain the criteria for being 'green'. These are a reverence for the Earth and all its creatures and a willingness to share the world's wealth among all its peoples. There should be harmony between people of every race, colour and creed. He wants a large-scale reduction in arms spending, a non-nuclear defence policy and a non-nuclear, low energy strategy based on conservation, greater efficiency and renewable resources. He seeks a rejection of materialism and the destructive values of industrialism, with the protection of the environment a precondition for a healthy society. He calls for the recognition of the crucial importance of signifi-cant reductions in population growth levels. He proposes that there should be open participatory democracy and an emphasis on self reliance, decentralised communities, personal growth and spiritual development.

The big danger at the moment is that the major parties will change a few of their policies and, like Margaret Thatcher, call themselves 'friends of the earth'. We need far more fundamental and far reach-ing changes in our world view.

GROWING OUT OF TROUBLE

There have been those from both the Right and the Left who have argued the importance of economic growth as a way of moving ahead. In *The Future of Socialism* Anthony Crosland argued that it was better for countries to work for economic growth rather than try to redistribute wealth. He said that while a redistribution of wealth would lead possibly to a ten per cent increase in wealth to the poor, the same could be achieved by only about 3% growth for three years.

Similar points were made by Wilfred Beckerman in his book *In Defence of Economic Growth*. He argued that a failure to maintain economic growth would mean continued poverty, deprivation, disease, squalor, degradation, slavery and soul-destroying toil for countless millions of the world's population.

He also suggested that all the poor countries of the world should reject the anti growth doctrine, in the knowledge that continued growth is not only essential in their own countries in order to eliminate poverty, but it is also important that the developed countries continue to grow in order to provide expanding markets for their products.

He gave evidence of the poor social conditions in London in the nineteenth century. When the French ambassador was travelling across London to take up his position in 1822, he talked of an 'immense skull cap of smoke which covers the city of London'. He argued that those who fashionably complain about the carbon monoxide poisoning from motor cars around Oxford Street might note that in the last century it was reported:

> 'The space bounded by Oxford Street, Portland Place, New Road, Tottenham Court Road, is one vast cesspool, the sewers being so imperfectly constructed that their contents are almost always stagnant... thousands of working men are closely confined for perhaps 14 or 15 hours a day out of the 24, in a room in which the offensive effluvium of some cesspool is mingling with the atmosphere'.

Beckerman stated that the social conditions were so bad that it was not surprising that there were very high deaths from typhus, tuberculosis and numerous other diseases associated with insanitary and unhealthy living conditions.

Beckerman called for a middle-of-the-road attitude towards growth. He suggested that extreme positions such as a rousing battle cry to keep up with the Japanese, or at the other end of the scale to stop the ravage of the earth until it is too late, do have an appeal. However, he proposed that an optimum solution is one that rightly appeals most to economists. He noted the population problem as *'one of the most urgent and serious problems to be faced by the world as a whole'* and he argued that it was more important than the pollution problem. He reported that some scientists were sufficiently optimistic about energy supplies that they believed the planet could support 20 billion people at current American living standards by using the virtually limitless resources that exist of atomic energy, water, air and the minerals locked up in common rock.

The weakness of this kind of argument is that it is purely speculative. The present reality is that people are hungry and we have pollution now. The oil reserves of countries like Britain are already dwindling. We need to begin to change our lifestyles immediately. If scientists do make some great discoveries in the future then all well and good, but we have the potential now to solve all our major problems with our current knowledge and we should use it.

THE WAY AHEAD

In this opening chapter I have set out the various problems and the fact that the current response to them is very much wanting. However, there are some hopeful signs that the politicians are becoming aware of the public's concern. There are indications that the politicians of both Left and Right are thinking seriously about such issues as the greenhouse effect and pollution. These, however, are only the first tentative steps in the right direction. There are few signs that governments are about to follow sensible policies on the issues of population increase and its effect on world poverty, or of a different approach to crime and health.

One of the major changes needed is a different approach to the economy and a move away from the idea of the need for growth as put forward by such as Crosland and Beckerman. In 1973, I collaborated with Bob Wharton, who was working with the Economist Intelligence Unit at the time, and we wrote an article entitled 'An International Social Index' for the *New Internationalist*. The article aimed to compare the quality of life in different countries based on a number of indicators which included the longevity of life and crime levels. It raised a number of issues about the relationship of economic growth to the quality of life.

In the Introduction we asked the questions that if Britain's economy grew by two per cent a year did it mean that the quality of life in Britain is two per cent better? Or if the average American is forty times wealthier than the average Kenyan did it follow that the USA is forty times better as a place to live. We continued to say that for most practical purposes, the world conducts its affairs as if the answers to these questions were 'Yes'. For government and international organisations are still using Gross National Product as a yardstick for measuring the quality of life and comparing the development of different nations. '*We know GNP isn't enough*' they say, '*but it's the only practical measuring stick that we've got* '.

We then measured the quality of life of six countries directly and drew up an international social index as an alternative to GNP and stated that we believed that there was an urgent need for a new emphasis on the quality of life rather than its distorted reflection in the warped mirror of economic growth.

To compile the index, a number of measures were used which included: the availability of the essentials of life, housing and working conditions, economic security, ease of communications, health, social stability, social freedom and availability of education.

The crucial problem to be solved was how to weight the different parts of the index, what measures we should use to make comparisons and how far our list of items was comprehensive. In the research we compared six countries. Three of them — Britain, United States and Holland — were rich and three of them — Brazil, Kenya and India — were relatively poor.

The findings of the study have important implications for future policy. What was clear from the data was that the three rich countries were much better off than the three poor countries, and between rich and poor there was a reasonable correlation between wealth and quality of life. However, amongst the three rich countries the relationship was much less clear. The United States was more than twice as rich as either Britain or Holland and yet it fared much worse in terms of social conditions. The average length of life in Holland was four years longer than the United States. The Dutch murder rate was only one-twelfth as high, yet the country had only a quarter of the proportion of its population in prison. The Dutch infant mortality rate was only 62% of that of the United States. The data also showed that, while Britain did not usually match up to the social conditions in Holland, nevertheless it was superior to the United States on nine of the ten indicators.

So the information showed that increased wealth was very important until a country had developed sufficiently. However, once it had reached a certain level there ceased to be much of a correlation between wealth and the quality of life. Once a certain level of wealth has been reached, it seemed to us the crucial factor was to use the wealth that had been obtained wisely rather than concentrate on producing more.

One point we stressed was that of the optimum. This is most easily seen by food production. If a Third World country is only able to provide half the necessary food requirement then clearly an increased quantity and quality of food is highly desirable. However, once the doubling of food production had occurred there would be little need to increase it further.

Japan's experience shows this very clearly. Between 1975 and 1986 its GNP more than doubled to over $16,000 per head. Yet its calorific consumption actually fell. The document *Japan 1988* suggests a calorific intake of 2,581 in 1985 compared to 3,647 for the United States (1982) and 2,401 for China (1979-81). However, rather than Japan increasing its food production, the data indicates that about one-quarter of the citizens of the United States are overweight and so

22

the society would benefit healthwise from a reduction in consumption.

So in this area growth is not necessarily desirable and in the next two chapters I discuss this issue in greater depth to show how poor an indicator wealth is of the quality of life and suggest that what is needed is a combination of growth in production in some areas, stability in other areas and a reduction in yet other areas.

CONCLUSION

This book does not aim to give people detailed suggestions on how to live their lives but offers recommendations on how society should change to allow greater freedom for individual development. Jobs should be made as interesting as possible, education should be responsive to the development of the personality, individuals should feel secure in the knowledge that the state will provide for them at vulnerable times in their life such as childhood, illness, childbirth and old age, and people should not suffer discrimination on the grounds of ethnic group, race, sex, or social class. The environment should be protected for ourselves and future generations, and there should be freedom of ideas whether political or religious.

So I will examine the economy and certain key areas such as education, health, crime and international relations including world poverty to suggest how to bring about the necessary changes in society.

Chapter 2

Higher Income for a Better Life. True or false?

The media in most countries proclaim the message that it's better to be wealthy. It praises Japan for its economic growth and the fact that in 1988 it overtook the United States as the richest major country in terms of income per head. Between 1970 and 1986, the number of passenger cars in Japan increased fourfold and the number of miles travelled by car more than doubled. The road space only increased by 11% so the overcrowding on the roads greatly increased. If this trend continues the problems will get worse.

Japan is used as an example to begin this chapter but subsequently it will be argued that similar problems are occurring all over the world. There follow twelve reasons why despite an increase in wealth in society there may be a decrease in the quality of life.

A major point is:

'In developed countries wealth is such a poor indicator of the quality of life that it needs to be abandoned and other criteria used.'

Twelve reasons why an increase in Gross National Product does not necessarily improve life.

THE DIFFERENCE BETWEEN OIL AND WATER

Traditionally economists treat oil and water as if they are the same kind of commodity but there is a large difference. If we waste water, it runs to the sea and will be evaporated by the sun and return as rain, if we waste oil it is gone forever.

This was one of the central points made by E F Schumacher in *Small is Beautiful*. Economists had failed to distinguish between income and capital. He argued that much of the wealth of the world was based not upon the production of new goods but on the consumption of the stock of wealth. To a traditional economist it might seem positive if demand grew for fossil fuels such as oil, gas or coal, measured wealth would be increased. However, Schumacher pointed out that once it is realised that fossil fuels are part of the world's stock of wealth, it becomes clear they should be approached differently. It is important that they are conserved and treated with the respect they deserve as irreplaceable assets.

Fossil fuels are past energy of the sun stored up. There have been a few politicians who have shown awareness of the potential problems for the future. In 1981 Henry Kissinger, in a lecture to the annual conference of state legislators, drew attention to a Gallup Poll which showed that less than half of the American public knew the country had to import oil and only 17% realised the extent of its dependence. He approved the attempts of the then president, Jimmy Carter, to reduce the consumption by 10% by 1985. Kissinger also pointed to the fact that in 1975 the United States *wasted* more fossil fuel than was used by two thirds of the world's population. So it is clear that a reduction of energy consumption could in fact benefit society.

There are those who question the fact that raw materials might be used up. Beckerman in his book *In Defence of Economic Growth* argues that such concerns are not new and draws attention, for example, to the fact that in 1908, President Theodore Roosevelt was alarmed at the impending exhaustion of mineral reserves. As far as oil is concerned Beckerman argues that, although there is considerable doubt about how much oil reserves might still be found, there are still vast areas of the world which have not been explored and that the oil under sea beds has as yet hardly been touched. He suggests that although oil may be the most vulnerable of the resources at present, this does not mean industry will grind to a halt but that *even the least successful nuclear power companies will find themselves able to sell off nuclear reactors more easily* (p224). As to the pollution problem of nuclear waste, he suggests that there may well be a breakthrough in technology which will prevent it being formed. He also speculates on other possibilities such as solar energy and sea bed resources.

Although Beckerman may be right and more fossil fuel may be found, he is much too calm about the issue. *The New York Times* (20 Aug. 1989) announced that the government had lowered its estimate of untapped and undiscovered American oil reserves by 40% due to the failure of promising drilling prospects. This lowered the life expectancy of US oil reserves at current production rates, disregarding oil shale and tar sand, from 37 years to 26 years. A government spokesman was quoted *'There clearly is a decline. This is all the more reason why we must proceed with a national energy strategy to contend with declining domestic production and increasing imports'.*

Britain has not found any sources comparable with the oil in the North Sea. The finite oil reserves are not just a theoretical constraint in the future but a problem now. There needs to be a change in energy and transport policy, an issue which is discussed in the next chapter.

THE WASTEMAKERS

When a product is first developed its sales are to first time buyers, but once the market becomes saturated, the number sold may fall dramatically, as happened in the 1950's with washing machines in Britain. Replacement demand is strongly influenced by the lifespan of the article in question, so manufacturers may be able to get extra profits by building obsolescence into their articles. No firms admit to this publicly. There are no advertisements along the lines 'Buy our light bulbs and soon come back for replacements'. On occasions it is possible to get inside information. When my father was a garage owner, he went to a seminar organised by the Motor Trade Communications Limited where Leo Domhill of *Glass's Guide,* the motor trades' definitive magazine on prices, compared the length of life of cars in Britain and the United States. He argued that for many years Britain had been making its cars last too long and there were too many old cars. However, he took heart from an increase in the scrappage rate:

> 'The average life of a car continues to shorten and there has been a most encouraging speed up in the scrappage rate over the past five years . . .
> It is expected that at least another 500,000 cars were scrapped during 1967 so that by the end of this year the great bulk of all cars of 1954 vintage and earlier will have been eliminated. At long last our scrappage rate is beginning to come within sight of the average 8½ p.a. that exists in the USA.'

There is clearly a conflict of interest in that people want their cars to last as long as possible and hence its worth on the used car market maintained. Yet those manufacturers seeking to maximise profits, against the greater good of the community, want the car to last as short a time as possible without facing adverse publicity.

Apart from built-in obsolescence, some companies may even take more direct action to maintain demand. A good example of what can happen is provided by the television industry in Britain. When black and white television was introduced, sales were good for a number of years until the market became saturated and then they fell off. When colour television was developed, the majority of British people decided to rent rather than buy. It might have been thought that, after a few years, there would have been a healthy market in second-hand televisions as the better-off sections of the community began to demand newer models.

I did not see much evidence of this happening so I went along with Professor John Stancer of Trent Polytechnic to see the chief accountant of one of the major British firms. I asked him if they ever sold off televisions which were too old to rent out. He said that if they sold older colour television sets, they would 'kill-off' their market. They therefore had a policy of destroying sets and had two factories to break up 250,000 colour sets each year. So the logic of the market meant that firms were spending their time breaking up television sets that were in perfect working order. What might a judge say to a vandal who had destroyed a colour television set? There would be lofty statements about the need to value property and much brow beating about the state of modern youth. Yet the profit motive under monopolistic competition means that television sets are destroyed on a regular basis. A student for a television destroyer told me that in Ireland, they had to keep a strict check on the parts to make sure that people weren't failing to break them all and instead recycling them for further use.

Some of the tricks manufacturers develop to sell more of their product can be amusing and Vance Packard in *The Waste Makers* gives the example of potato peelers. These do not wear out, yet enough are sold every two years to put one in every US home. A colour consultant explained to a meeting in New York an ingenious scheme which a client had thought up for increasing sales. He drew attention to the fact that potato peelers never wear out but investigation reveals that the peelers get thrown away with the potato peelings. So one of his colleagues came up with a dazzling plan for helping along this throw-away process. He proposed that their company should paint its peelers a colour as much like a potato peeling as possible. However, a potato-coloured peeler wouldn't have much eye appeal on the sales counter so they decided to resolve that problem by displaying the peeler on a colourful card. Once the peeler was taken home and the bright card removed, the chances that the peeler would be lost were excellent.

So there are many ways in which the demand for products can be kept artificially high. However, this is not really wealth and in many areas there is a great deal of waste. There is a waste of resources, a waste of people's time and in many ways, a lower standard of service to the consumer.

THE WANT MAKERS

28 Advertising can, in many instances, be informative and useful. It

places people in contact with the services they need. It has value for governments when there is a need for public information programmes and many advertisements are relatively innocuous. However, there is a strong negative side. The first point is that many goods do not suffer from physical obsolescence so advertisers therefore looked at the possibility of creating psychological obsolescence. Vance Packard in *The Wastemakers* reported a conference of the sellers of gas appliances at which the conferees were exhorted to follow the car manufacturers in striving to make people ashamed of having equipment which was more than two or three years old. An executive told the conference with enthusiasm that what makes the United States great is the creation of wants and desires, the creation of dissatisfaction with the old and outmoded.

This creation of wants from an objective sense is, at best, a waste of time and at worst a negative influence for all those who feel guilty at not being able to afford the product. There could be problems for society if the ideas of change and moving on to new things permeates from material goods into personal relationships. For if this happens, then it could lead to people seeking new relationships and to an even higher divorce rate.

There has always been a cultural difference between Britain and the United States on this matter. One of the most interesting pamphlets to come from the Second World War was that written by Margaret Mead to the British people to try and help them understand the American servicemen and to reduce some of the tension between them. The pamphlet *The American Troops and the British Community* pointed out that sometimes problems occurred because large numbers of American troops looking for a good time were stationed near small villages. She pointed to other conflicts of norms. For example, the British placed great store on people standing upright and regarded it as a sign of spinelessness and indiscipline to slouch. In contrast the Americans saw 'no harm in taking the weight off their feet by leaning against the nearest wall in sight'. She explained differences in the sexual norms but, more importantly, pointed out the fact that America was a relatively new country which could not value things that were old and so instead concentrated on the new. The servicemen wanted things now and wanted them fashionable and up to date.

This cultural difference has continued to a degree and the desire for change and new things may well be one of the reasons that the divorce rate in the United States is well above that of comparable European countries. Advertising, of course, encourages such values.

A slightly different point is that advertising can create fears in society. An article in *New Society* (16 Feb. 1984) discussed the way that people have been bombarded with concern about body odour (BO) since the 1920's. It seems it is worse for women to smell like women than for men to smell like men, for 84% of British women used deodorant compared to less than half of British men (46%). In fact British advertisers had a problem with the men and in the five years up to 1983, the sales of men's talcum powder halved.

Bald is beautiful

Advertisers have had continuing success with adverts for men's wigs or transplants and newspapers continue to spill out the message that when men lose their hair it is a great tragedy. This creation of norms whereby perfectly normal things, such as a man losing his hair, are made to seem abnormal and stigmatised, is a problem for societies. An article *A group where less means more* published in the *New York Times* (9 Nov. 1988) states that according to the American Hair Loss Council in Tyler, Texas, there are 30 million men who are bald or balding. When he was rejected for a job on the grounds he was too bald to look dynamic, John. T. Capps 3rd made a list of all the balding men he knew and sent them letters inviting them to join the Bald Headed Men of America, which now has over 20,000 members. Mr Capps spreads his message with such slogans as 'The Lord is just the Lord is fair. He gave some brains the others hair'. He also commented 'baldness is mind over matter. It doesn't matter if the person doesn't mind'. So if this kind of movement keeps growing there will be a transfer of resources as measured by sales of hair pieces and wigs and yet an improvement in that many bald men will have an improved self-image and will not see the need to waste time and energy disguising their baldness.

Possessions lead to happiness?

There are three major problems with advertising. The first one is the continuing message that 'possessions lead to happiness'. The idea is put forward, either implicitly or explicitly, that if you own the latest model of car, the most up-to-date fashions and buy the most up-to-date furniture, then this will make you happy. This general propaganda is reinforced by many television programmes such as 'Sale of the Century' where a whole range of goods are on offer. The whole message is that everyone should want these items and to congratulate those who are lucky enough to be on the programme to win many prizes. As I said in Chapter One, we need to be moving away from this over-concern with owning and moving instead towards a society where people are really living. People should be valued for what they are, what they do and who they help and not what they own.

A second problem is that advertising distorts consumption patterns.

This is a particular problem in the United States where advertising appears on television every few minutes. Advertising can cause problems to people who have problems. The continued advertising of food products in a society where a high percentage of people are unhealthily overweight clearly creates difficulties as does the advertising of alcohol to those who are trying to abstain. The use of sexual images to sell may create feelings of relative deprivation amongst some people. The pushing of the idea that women in particular should be slim may well be a factor in leading to anorexia.

One important point is that if nobody is going to make money from a product it will not be advertised and consequently there is a danger that a bad commercial product can take over from a good natural process. A good example is the decline in breastfeeding in the United States. Babies fed on breast milk receive their mother's immunity from various diseases and are less likely to suffer from gastroenteritis. The War on Want book (*The Baby Killer Scandal*) quotes research indicating that twenty-nine out of thirty women are able to breastfeed. The advertising companies set out to change habits and successfully reduced breastfeeding. The number of women breastfeeding declined from seven out of ten (72%) in 1931-5 to three out of ten (29%) in 1971-3. This decrease was especially marked among blacks, the poor and the less-well educated women. It seems that the more deprived the group, the less able they were to see through the misinformation.

A study conducted among Indians on reservations in Canada in 1962 showed the major diseases killing babies were gastroenteritis and tuberculosis, and that simply by bringing babies up on the breast rather than on the bottle, it would have been possible to reduce the mortality rate of Indian babies by one third. More recent evidence raises other questions. Milk powders were first shown to be a cause of aluminium toxicity in 1985, when two babies who died in America were found to have huge amounts of aluminium in their brains. The *Sunday Times* (20 November 1988) carried an article *Research shows danger in baby bottle milk.* This argued that surveys have shown that milk powders are often contaminated with aluminium and deliver at least 100 times more than breast milk. It seems the danger period may be the first few days or weeks of life before the body's mechanisms for guarding against such toxins develop.

The advice 'Breast is best', particularly during this early period, is reinforced by the evidence that even relatively small amounts of aluminium can affect the brain once it gets into the bloodstream. It interferes with the production of enzymes vital to cerebral activity. There are also fears that high exposure in babyhood could accelerate mental decline in old age. Clear links have also been established between aluminium and Alzheimer's disease, a form of dementia affecting more than 500,000 Britons. Areas with raised levels of aluminium in drinking water have 50-100% more patients with the disease.

In the developed world the advantages of breast milk began to receive publicity so that by 1978 in the United States the percentage of women breastfeeding was up to 47%, an improvement but well below the level that would be best for the overall health of American babies.

To their great shame many of the companies expanded their activities into the Third World. In Chile 95% of one year-olds were being breastfed in 1955 but by 1970 it was down to only 20% even at two months with the resulting detriment to the children's health. Senator Edward Kennedy hit the spot in 1978 when he said *'Can a product which requires clean water, good sanitation, adequate family income and literate parents to follow printed instructions, be properly used in areas where the water is contaminated, sewage runs in the streets, poverty is severe and illiteracy is high?'*

To be fair, the representatives of the companies may not always be aware of the problems they are causing. Dr Elizabeth Hillman, a paediatrician on the staff of the Kenyatta National Hospital in Nairobi, Kenya, described how the Nestlé representatives went to visit them at the hospital to ask if they had any opinion about the War on Want publication *The Baby Killer.* They were told there was a child that had been fed on Nestlé's milk who was nearly dying in the emergency ward. As she took the two representatives in to see the baby it collapsed and died. She had to leave the two men and help with the resuscitation procedure which proved unsuccessful. After the baby was pronounced dead she said, *'We all watched the mother turn away from the dead baby and put the can of Nestlé's milk in her bag before she left the ward.'* She further commented that it was a vivid demonstration of the effects of bottle feeding because the mother was perfectly capable of breastfeeding. The two men walked out of the room, very pale, shaken, quiet and clearly shocked by what they had seen.

In 1984 Nestlé's agreed to scale back its aggressive advertising campaign. However the *New York Times* (3 Sept 1989) reported that the issue is resurfacing in the United States as Bristol Myers were about to begin a multi-million dollar advertising campaign. Doctors were very critical of the decision because it is likely to lead to fewer poor women breastfeeding with the resultant increase in infant deaths.

One general problem is that advertising has concentrated on persuading people to use labour-saving devices and this has led to a general lack of exercise. In 1972 I set out the problem of the increased mechanisation of life as follows:

This has meant that a number of people do not get enough exercise and have to diet or listen to exercises given out each day on the radio stations. I often feel that if the advertisers had their way, then we would all be sitting down while mechanical diggers dug the gardens, mechanical toothbrushes brushed our teeth and mechanical washer-uppers washed up for us. A minimum time would be spent in producing 'instant food'. Of course as no exercise would be taken by the people measuring up to the advertiser's dreams, they would have to buy cycling machines in order to get exercise, or to diet to make sure they lost weight.

Since then there have been a few attempts to moderate behaviour in the opposite direction, largely at the request of the medical profession. The number of heart attacks has reduced as people have become increasingly aware of the value of exercise and the need for a more balanced diet. In most Western countries there has been an increase in the number of people doing exercise by aerobics or jogging. These developments are welcome but they have not really come to grips with the scale of the problem. It is only a small, if visible, minority which is getting enough exercise. Few people conduct their lives so that proper exercise is a natural part of it. I asked the man in a sports shop why people buy an exercise bicycle rather than a real one which was not only the same price but would also take them places. He said the advantage of his bicycle was that people would not get tired and stranded a long way from home. Often the traffic is so dangerous that people cannot safely cycle or the weather conditions may be adverse. However, it would be more beneficial if we could create a society where exercise occurred more naturally as part of everyday living.

Money Can't Buy You Love

The old adage that the best things in life are free still applies but it is true that we need enough cash so that we can visit our friends, renew acquaintances and be free from many worries. However, money should be the servant and not the controller of our lives. The continuing impact of advertising on us suggests that the most important thing is to own goods and that happiness can be purchased. For example, one advertisement says that 'Happiness is a cigar called Hamlet'. Although we may understand the advertiser's desire to sell, this creates the impression that happiness can be bought. The reality of life is that things such as good health and the development of personality and relationships are more important and cannot be bought.

WASTE NOT WANT WHAT?

The movement towards disposable goods gives a false impression of the increase in wealth and leads to waste and pollution. In a major article discussing the trend to disposable goods the New York Times (31 May 1987) reported that Japan had introduced a throwaway camera and Fuji had sold 1.5 million in six months. It discussed the merits of the two kinds of disposable camera about to be sold in the United States. It also reported other innovations such as the throwaway travel iron, the throwaway fluorescent light and throwaway phones which have a lifespan of under a year. The article quoted Edward Cornish, President of the World Future Society in Bethesda as saying 'We'll see prefabricated homes that will be manufactured from inexpensive materials and will be thrown out and replaced rather than repaired'. He also suggested that homes could have detachable rooms which could be disposed of and new ones attached already fitted out with the comforts of modern living.

The article suggested that one reason for the trend was the rise in the two-income family which produced a higher income for people but less time to spend it. It also pointed out that there was a dark side to the throwaway boom because metal producing industries were depressed and there were environmental problems with non biodegradable plastics making up 8% of US waste. It also pointed out that when burned, many plastics give off toxic fumes and others contribute to acid rain. An economist was quoted in the article as saying that it would be fairer if manufacturers had to pay the price of adequately disposing of plastic razors rather than the cost being borne by the community.

The article did not raise the more important issue of whether we really want a disposable society. People are not short of time. The average person watches over twenty-four hours of television a week, therefore it would seem they have a great deal of time which could be used in other ways. The question is rather one of ideology. At my college they introduced food on throwaway plates. This was objectionable on numerous grounds — environmental, aesthetic and financial. It was abandoned when the students discovered the costs of the disposable plates were so high they were being washed and re-used.

Disposable goods are wrong for at least three reasons. First, we do not want a rubbish-making society. We must work towards improving the environment without leaving garbage around for future generations. Secondly, because disposable goods are of such poor quality — society should be working towards making quality goods which will stand the test of time. Thirdly, the growth in disposable goods does not make economic sense because it wastes resources. The goods also impose the external cost of garbage disposal which is not borne by the consumer or producer.

34

Where do we put our rubbish?

This leads us to the question of waste disposal. The issue came to the fore in the public's mind in 1987 when a barge from Islip Long Island tried to dump its load of festering rubbish. It floated around for 162 days trying to deposit in various countries and states before the rubbish was incinerated in Brooklyn and the remains returned home. The question of rubbish disposal has become very important in the United States and rightly so for there are numerous problems that result from it. One problem is that land dumps are rapidly filling up. The United States produces about twice as much rubbish per head as other developed countries. A *New York Times* report of June 1987 said that London produced 6,831 tons of rubbish a day compared to 14,329 in New York.

In New York, two thirds of the state's dumps are expected to close by 1997 and overall in the US, over half the states will use up most of their garbage landfills before the end of the century. Few new sites are being developed. There have been several reports in the United States where the local community has been unable to accept garbage. One in 1988 told of people disposing of their rubbish by putting it in Salvation Army clothing drops. One plan suggested in the summer of 1988 was to bring the rubbish to Britain and place it in the disused tin mines in Cornwall. However, the United States took note of protests by local residents.

The United States is not the only country with problems. In Japan, residents are required by law to separate their garbage into the rubbish which will burn and that which will not. This clearly reduces the volume, however, it is estimated that Tokyo will run out of space for garbage by 1995. Of course, if items such as disposable cameras become more popular, this date might have to be brought forward. There have been some developments in the US which give cause for optimism. Connecticut and New Jersey have passed recycling laws. New Jersey requires residents to separate materials such as glass and newspapers from the trash and to recycle at least 25% of all household garbage to save space in the land fills. A study found that the countries that introduced recycling were in fact saving money. In Philadelphia a law was passed which insisted that residents separate their trash into various categories.

A report in *Newsday* (20 Aug. 1989) described developments in Wellesley, Mass. In 1971 a town environmental group, 'Action for Ecology', began campaigning for recycling. Now 83% of residents take their garbage to the Recycling Disposal Facility and 90% of those separate recyclable materials from other waste. The plant provides residents with neatly lettered bins for newspapers, magazines, aluminium foil, cardboard, milk cartons, plastic bottles of certain colour and sizes and a bin for simple household garbage. In addition, there is a Goodwill Industries Trailer for old clothing and a 'Take it or leave it' section where residents leave items they think someone else can use.

In July 1988, Suffolk County on Long Island passed a law which banned plastic grocery bags and many plastic food containers. In August 1989 I interviewed Bill Roefch who was helping Brookhaven comply with a ban on burying rubbish that was coming into effect in December 1990 because of a shortage of land fills. He told me the town aimed to recycle, re-use and to form garbage compost. It is proposed that the material the town cannot treat in this way be transformed into an energy source.

Other places are also taking action. In Old Bethpage, Long Island an organisation called RAGE — Residents Against Garbage Expansion — prepared a plan to turn autumn leaves into organic compost.

New York and various other states now have a law which insists on a deposit on beer containers which are then recycled and there are proposals to extend this to cover the use of wine bottles. Some plastic bottles are also recycled. These kinds of developments are to be applauded as ecologically sound, economically wise and aesthetically superior.

Apart from the sheer volume of rubbish, there are problems with pollution as the following points show.

In 1987, a Congressional report found that there were at least 1,882 potentially hazardous waste sites on Federal property. The US Office of Technology Assessment produced a report which said that a new Federal programme was needed to reduce industrial production of hazardous waste by up to 50% in the subsequent five years.

Styroform, used by the large fast food places, is damaging the ozone level. This led to the *New York Times* amongst others calling for McDonalds to replace it with wrappings made from recyclable paper. Other items that lead to potentially great quantities of hazardous waste are old batteries, plastic bags and newspapers.

There is a great problem with indestructible plastic waste. It was found in New Jersey that half the sea turtles that arrived in the state's waters died of plastic pollution.

In February 1988, the US army and Shell agreed to pay as much as a billion dollars to clean up the waste site near Denver which is one of the most contaminated in the United States with the residues of nerve gases and chemical weapons.

There is concern that pollution from dumps will leak into water supplies. Also the burning of rubbish leads to pollutants such as lead, cadmium dioxin and other toxic substances being introduced into the air. The move towards disposable items in recent years can be seen, therefore, to greatly inflate the Gross National Product. A move back to real cups, plates and containers would not only reduce waste, it would also increase the quality of living.

KEEPING UP WITH THE JONESES

Many goods carry a large status element and, while they may enhance an individual's self image, do not necessarily contribute to the general quality of life. For example if a person buys a quality car because of its smooth ride and general quality, then it is of benefit. However, if it is purchased for the purpose of being 'ahead' of the rest of the population, then from society's point of view there is no benefit because the positive aspects of status will only be valid if matched by deprivation amongst others. Americans call the process of maintaining status striving to 'live up to the Joneses'. By skilful manipulation, advertisers have presented the purchase of goods not only as a necessity but also as a means of avoiding social censure.

Packard pointed out that from at least the early 1950's, merchandisers in the United States have been particularly interested in women in the middle income brackets who make up 65% of the population in a typical community and have a control of a large part of the country's purchasing power. They geared advertising to their needs. The advertisers found that the woman they called 'Mrs middle majority' was simply delighted by products associated with the kitchen and that her kitchen was likely to be better equipped than a so-called 'upper class' kitchen. The advertisers set out to convince her that pride in her kitchen and home in general should be her main priority and source of status. As far as the equipment was concerned she should have the most up-to-date. Packard describes a lecture in which the director of American Color Trends complained about the fact that many housekeepers had the attitude that 'any old piece of equipment will do so long as it works'. He went on to explain that by setting up fashions in colour it would help increase the obsolescence of appliances.

There is little doubt that the United States was ahead of Britain and other countries in using consumer research to find ways of increasing sales, but this is now growing on both sides of the Atlantic. In Britain there has been a strong emphasis on 'designer' kitchens and it is now generally accepted that many appliances should be replaced long before they have reached the end of their useful lives.

This is now particularly true of cars. In 1963, British number plates started to display a letter indicating the year of manufacture. At first the letter was changed in January of each year but demand for new cars fell towards the end of the year so in 1967, the letters were changed at the beginning of August. This had the desired effect of increasing car sales at the end of the summer and in August 1970 a garage in North London put up a sign 'Are you a J Man?' This encouraged the idea that last year's models were now inferior and old-fashioned.

WASTEFUL DISTRIBUTION OF WEALTH

In a better world, the necessities of life-food, clothing, shelter and health care would be produced for all before luxury goods were produced for the few.

One of the problems with economics is that, although an item can be produced and money made available to buy it, that does not necessarily make it socially desirable. Some economists would argue that this does not much matter, as the production of frivolous goods is dependent on demand and, if someone is willing to pay, why should any value judgements be made.

However, Tawney made an important point in *The Acquisitive Society* originally published just after the First World War. He argued that since the demand of one income of £50,000 is as powerful a magnet as the demand of 500 incomes of £100, it diverts energy from the creation of wealth to the multiplication of luxuries. On the world level this results in rich countries producing luxury goods of relatively little importance while the poor do not have enough purchasing power to buy food. So much of what is produced and called wealth, is, strictly speaking waste, because it consists of articles which, though reckoned as part of income, are not necessities. Luxury goods should only be produced once there is a sufficiency of goods necessary for living.

If people could choose world priorities for expenditure most would agree that all children should be adequately fed and housed within a warm network of social relationships. This is apparent from appeals such as that organised by Bob Geldof. However on a world level the unequal distribution of expenditure is obvious. For example, vast amounts are spent on armaments while governments give only a pittance to help the poor countries. Furthermore, very often the poor receive little, if any, help from the richer elements within their own country. So there is much scope for change.

POLLUTION AND ITS SIDE EFFECTS

Most economic and social activities have side effects which are not measured in monetary terms. People are advised not to swim in many rivers or streams because of pollution. Acid rain has destroyed all life in some northern and Scottish lakes and rivers. The recognition of the effects of discharging sulphurous substances into the atmosphere has led to the Scandinavian countries, Denmark, Finland, Iceland, Norway and Sweden reaching agreement with West Germany, France and the Soviet Union to reduce the amount of such emission by about 30% over the ten years until 1994. There have been attempts to persuade Britain to join the agreement *(Guardian* 2 March 1984)

One of the most disturbing long-term trends in terms of pollution is likely to be the continuous build-up of radioactive waste. This often has a half-life of 1,000 years and so as the oil runs out and coal stocks become depleted, there will be a strong pressure to rely on nuclear energy, even if the longer term damage to life cannot be prevented. One of the few British and United States politicians to take the issue seriously is the Labour Member of Parliament, Giles Radice. In 1979 he pointed out that the supplies of North Sea oil would decline by the 1990's and went on to say:

'At present the only assured source of fuel supply in the long term, apart from coal, is nuclear power. Because of the limited availability of uranium, dependence on nuclear power almost certainly involves major reliance on fast reactors about which the Royal Commission on Environmental Pollution has expressed concern on social, environmental and security grounds. It will also be impossible to ignore the energy needs and decisions of other countries, including the developing countries'.

In Britain the nuclear industry has been influencing public opinion with a series of advertisements in order to try and reduce public concern. One which appeared in the *Mail on Sunday* put forward a series of fiction and facts. That last two 'facts' deserve questioning:

FICTION. *We've got enough oil and coal to last us thousands of years.*
FACT. No we haven't. The world's existing oil reserves could run out in around 60 years. Even Britain's coal could run out in as little as 100 years. Not long when we think of our children's lifetimes.
FICTION. *Even if coal and oil do run out, they'll think of something else.*
FACT. It is possible that the various other energy sources such as wind power, wood and solar power will be developed but this has yet to happen in a significant way.
FICTION. *Wind, wave and tidal power are alternatives to nuclear electricity.*
FACT. In time, they will have a valuable role to play in helping to meet our energy needs but it is unlikely that they will ever be major contributors. The energy is often limited by nature and uneconomical to exploit. So it makes sense to look at something else.
FICTION. *You will get cancer if you live near a nuclear electricity station.*
FACT. On the contrary a recent independent study shows that cancer death rates are, if anything, lower than the national average around nuclear electricity stations.

It continued to urge that *'There are now over 400 commercial reactors worldwide. And in a modern world we just have to keep up or we risk becoming a third rate power'.*

This advertisement draws attention to the important fact that the Western countries in particular are using up the resources of the world at a rapid rate which cannot go on indefinitely. However, there are grave doubts about the claims that cancer death rates are lower. Here is my letter to the British Advertising Standards Authorities.

16 December 1988

Dear Advertising Authority,

I have noted that during the month of November the Nuclear Power Industry had been placing numerous full page advertisements in British newspapers including the Mail On Sunday. This advertisement claims that it is a fiction that people will get cancer if they live near a nuclear power station and states that 'A recent independent study shows that cancer death rates are, if anything, lower than the national average around nuclear electricity stations.'

It seems to me that this statement is misleading and breaches the advertising code. The Guardian newspaper (2nd October 1987) drew attention to a report in the British Medical Journal which confirmed the excess in cases of leukamia among children living in Seascale a village neighbouring on a nuclear plant. Overall the cancer death rate in the village for children was three times that expected. The New York Times (21 May 1987) similarly reported a Massachussets Public Health Department study of men living near a new nuclear reactor in Plymouth which found an excess of over 50% of some kinds of cancers. This latter report led to the United States National Institutes of Health setting up a study of 'leukamia clusters' near nuclear power stations. (NYT 5 February 1988).

I would like to hear what action you propose to take in this case.

Yours sincerely

Dr Colin Francome

They replied on 20th January 1989 in a letter headed *private and confidential* stating that they had carefully considered the complaint and that, while they appreciated the anxieties, they believed that the advertisement would only be understood as representing one view of the public debate. They believed that as a non-elected body it would not be wise *to seek to hinder advertisers' freedom to express their views within this discussion, so long as what is being expressed is indeed a political opinion.*

So this means that the advertisers were free to tell lies, as it was a political advertisement. To prove it, they sent me a copy of their code which, under 'Political Advertisements', stated that to the extent that any advertiser expresses the advertiser's position on a matter of political controversy, neither the opinions expressed *nor any evidence which may be adduced in support of them are subject to the provisions of this code.*

It is, therefore, perfectly possible to lie in political adverts without being subject to the usual provisions. This raises very wide issues. The public can be lulled into a sense of security by the large-scale advertising of the major companies while any doubts raised are likely to be by relatively poor researchers whose evidence will probably receive little publicity.

The ex-Prime Minister, Harold MacMillan, used to criticise the selling off of the national assets in Britain as if we were selling off the family jewellery. The implication was that Britain was living beyond its means. A far more important loss for Britain, since the early Seventies, is the great stock of wealth in its North Sea oil. This will largely have been used up before the end of the century and in real terms Britain will then be much poorer. This consideration is important for the world as a whole in terms of the depletion of resources.

As far as the safety of nuclear power is concerned we must all have our grave doubts. It is highly unlikely that those responsible for the advertisement quoted will be taking their annual holidays in Chernobyl. There are three different areas of risk. First is the risk of accidents and this was the reason that the nuclear power station Lilco built on Long Island was not even opened. It was realised that if an accident did occur the Island would be impossible to evacuate.

Secondly there is the problem of disposal of radioactive waste. Mishan pointed out that in a fully developed US nuclear economy, some 200,000 pounds of plutonium will be generated annually. Bearing in mind that its half-life is about 24,000 years; and that a mere half-pound if it, dispersed into the atmosphere as fine insoluble particles, would be sufficient to inflict every living mortal with lung cancer, the plutonium 'inventory' that accumulated over the years would constitute a carcinogenic hazard for 1,000 human generations. Paul Brown, writing in *The Guardian* (12 Jan 1990) said that if you asked scientists who were involved at the start of the nuclear power industry how they imagined the industry would get rid of its waste, their reply would have been they trusted science would provide an answer. However, forty years on we are no nearer finding a solution. There are therefore good reasons why the United States has not opened any nuclear power stations for a number of years. In Britain, when the Government wanted to privatise the electricity industry, it had to pull nuclear reactors out of the sale.

The use of fossil fuels is leading to the accumulation of carbon dioxide and other gases in the atmosphere and to the warming up of the Earth. By 1989 the five hottest years worldwide this century were 1980, 1981,1983, 1987 and 1988. In the first part of 1988, average world temperatures were higher than at any point over the past 130 years. Friends of the Earth predict that the present best estimate of the rise in temperature is 3 degrees centigrade by the year 2030 which will take the world to temperatures it has not known for two million years. The warming so far has already led to melting of the ice caps and sea levels are over 10 centimetres higher that they were in 1900. As global warming continues to take effect scientists predict rises of as much as 1.65 metres by 2030. David Everest, formerly scientific officer for environmental pollution, is concerned that the rise in temperature could lead to the ice in the Antartic breaking off and falling into the sea — like ice cubes into a full glass — leading to surges where water would rise by as much as five metres.

In the United States, the Environmental Protection Agency reported in October 1988 that the effect will force major changes in society in the next century as the Earth heats up, farmlands dry out and coastal regions flood. The report continued to say that the ultimate effects will be irreversible and last for centuries. It argued that if change is slow enough nature can adapt through migration and society can adjust. A rapid climate change, however, may overwhelm the ability of systems to adapt. It said the cost of protecting major US cities from the changes could reach $111 billion by the year 2100. Even with the major cities protected, 7,000 square miles of land would be lost. Up to 25% of crops would be lost in southern areas that become too hot to farm, but northern areas are likely to become more productive.

In Britain a rise in sea levels will leave some towns like Blackpool as islands. Also according to the *Sunday Times* (1 Nov 1988) the sea could be washing through the streets of Canvey Island, Bristol, Avonmouth, Cardiff, Hull, Portsmouth, Morecambe, Great Yarmouth, Lowestoft and Felixstowe. Much of London would be flooded and the Thames barrier would be inadequate if sea levels were to rise by two metres. Already sea walls are being built in East Anglia at great cost and an estimate from Friends of the Earth predicts that the total cost of sea defences to protect the United Kingdom would be £8 billion. The *Sunday Times* has calculated that the cost of rebuilding the Thames Barrier alone would be £5 billion at 1988 prices.

Other countries too would face great problems. The Maldive Islands in the Indian Ocean barely reach two metres above sea level. They would be largely flooded.

The main single cause of the greenhouse effect is carbon dioxide gas produced by the burning of fossil fuels. It still comprises only 0.03% of the atmosphere in volume although its level has risen by 25% since the industrial revolution. It allows the short wave radiation from the sun to penetrate the Earth and then traps some of the longer wave length radiation that would otherwise be emitted from the Earth into the atmosphere. The concentration of carbon dioxide has increased from 315 parts per million in 1958 to 350 ppm in 1988 and is still climbing. Half of all the carbon dioxide emitted since the industrial revolution is still in the atmosphere today. The uncontrolled deforestation of the rainforests is another cause of the increase in CO_2. The trees would have absorbed CO_2 as they grew.

One of the most effective ways of reducing the greenhouse effect is energy conservation which, while reducing measured wealth, will nevertheless help to protect the environment. Japan's consumption of energy is only about half the level of the United States despite the fact that it has greatly increased its number of cars.

Chlorofluorocarbon (CFC) gases used in aerosol sprays, packaging, refrigeration and air conditioning are potent greenhouse gases. They trap 10,000 times as much heat as a molecule of CO_2 and remain active in the upper atmosphere for up to a hundred years. Methane gas is also important and levels have been rising rapidly and more than doubled since pre-industrial times.

The 1987 Montreal Protocol recommended a reduction of 50% in CFC's by the turn of the century but the European ministers in March 1989 called for an 85% reduction. In Britain, nearly two thirds of CFC's were in aerosol cans which were phased out at the end of 1989. Half of the rest is in fast food packaging and about a tenth is due to refrigerators — substitutes are available for both.

The Ozone Layer

The protective layer in the atmosphere absorbs damaging ultraviolet radiation from the sun. It is thinning out at a dangerous rate. The hole over the Antartic has grown to such a degree that there has been a 40% reduction in the springtime ozone in the decade to 1988. It will lead to an epidemic of skin cancers and also be damaging to may other life forms including cereals, fibre crops and sensitive marine organisms. The damage is being caused by CFC's — they have caused a hole in the sky which is growing and is currently the size of the United States. The use of CFC's in aerosol sprays was banned in the USA in 1978.

Currently the amount of CFC's released into the atmosphere is six times that which can be absorbed. To stabilise the ozone layer at the current level an 85% reduction in CFC's is needed. In addition to the phasing out of ozone 'unfriendly' cans, Friends of the Earth have drawn attention to companies such as McDonalds, Kentucky, Wimpy and Spud U Like who have agreed to stop using CFC's as blowing agents for hamburger cartons. Furthermore most supermarkets phased out CFC's in their egg boxes and meat trays by the end of 1988.

Transport and Pollution

Car transport is an important part of the pollution problem. Living in North London I see traffic jams just at the time that children are going to school. The lead fumes must be causing great damage to their brain development. Yet the build up of cars using leaded petrol has continued. There is also the problem of smell and the noise and the danger of accidents. Unburned hydrocarbons are a matter of concern because of their long term carcinogenic consequences. One test used to evaluate the cancer causing properties of materials is the AMES test which measures the capacity of pollutants to induce changes in the genetic code of bacteria. The Swedish Environmental Protection Board showed that diesel engine emissions are ten times as mutagenic as emissions from petrol driven engines which in turn are ten times more mutagenic than engines running on unleaded fuel and with catalytic converters. These 'cats' are sophisticated boxes fitted into the exhaust system. A three-way converter changes such gases as carbon monoxide and nitrogen oxides into carbon dioxide, nitrogen and water. They are mandatory in Japan and USA.

A 1986 study showed that London taxi drivers and drivers of other diesel-powered vehicles, had higher rates of bladder cancer. Similarly a study in the United States involving 25 states and corrected for smoking, occupation, and age, found those living in cities still had higher rates of lung cancer than those living in towns. Those living in towns had higher rates than those in rural areas. About 12% of lung cancer deaths were estimated to be due to the atmospheric pollution of urban residence. This is despite the fact that US controls are more strict than those in Europe.

Attempts to persuade the European Community to achieve equivalence with the US emission standards have not been successful due largely to the opposition by such countries as Britain. The compromise reached at Luxembourg in December 1987 allowed small cars to emit three times the pollutants as in the United States. Only 10% of the largest cars with engine sizes greater than two litres are required to have 3-way catalytic converters.

Air transport produces problems of noise which does not count as a negative factor in measuring wealth. One evening at Kenwood in Hampstead, London, during an open air concert, about three thousand people had their evening punctuated by a succession of planes flying over. If travel increases and the number of planes double or become noisier in the pursuit of faster travel, higher profits may be achieved at the expense of an increased adverse impact on people's lives.

Few consumer organisations in Britain and the USA have been able to make much impact but in France, those who live near airports have received compensation. In 1973 a levy was introduced based on the number of passengers in an aircraft and in the following ten years home owners near the major Paris airport received about £15 million compensation. UK airports do pay for noise insulation but this is only a minor relief.

Water Pollution

In 1989 the *Sunday Times* ran a campaign against river pollution in Britain. It reported that Britain's rivers were being polluted at a faster rate than at any time since records began. Pollution is so serious that ten per cent of rivers cannot support fish. One third of the industrial effluent samples tested by the Severn Trent Water Authority in 1988 were illegal as were a quarter of the industrial and sewage samples taken by the Yorkshire Water Authority. The increase in pollution in 1989 was the greatest since records began in 1958. The increase in pollution has killed tens of thousands of fish, mainly by oxygen starvation. There is also a threat to health as 70% of the UK drinking water is derived from rivers or, in the case of Wales and Scotland, rivers and lakes. The other 30% comes from underground supplies.

A quarter of all water pollution is unexplained. Of the remainder, industry caused half and among the leading law breakers were some of the major companies chaired by some of Britain's most respected business people. The remaining half was caused more or less equally by water authorities via their sewage works and by farmers who allow waste to seep into rivers.

One of the problems with water pollution is the level of nitrates which are toxic when present in excessive amounts in drinking water. It leads to a reduction in oxygen uptake in the lungs and is particularly harmful to babies. It also combines with the amines in our food to form substances called N-nitrosamines which have been shown to cause cancer in 39 animal species including primates and has led to speculation that it may lead to stomach cancer in humans. So far the results have been contradictory with only some high nitrate areas having excess cases of stomach cancer. However, because the drinking water in many areas of Britain has nitrate levels above the safe guidelines laid down by the EEC, in December 1986 Friends of the   *45*

Earth reported the Government to the European Commission. This led to it being forced to take action.

The increased use of nitrogen fertiliser is a contributory factor to the pollution of rivers, lakes and groundwaters.

Air Pollution

Evidence given to the British government in 1988 by Friends of the Earth stated that its concept of pollution had changed from identifying isolated examples of damage to investigating the way that whole ecosystems break down under the accumulation of air pollutants. It maintained that air pollution damage has been identified in virtually all plant and animal groups. While fresh water is being polluted by air, nature reserves will not survive. The evidence went on to say that some pollutants had been reduced, such as the emission of sulphur dioxide (SO_2), the major cause of acid rain. However, it was still at too high a high level and countries such as Sweden have complained about the effect of Britain's acid rain on their trees. In fact, the British government has officially taken responsibility for the damage. The Nordic Council of 1986 called for a short term reduction in sulphur dioxide emission of 80% and a longer term fall of 90%. Other pollutants such as nitrogen oxides, ozone and ammonia have increased and carbon monoxide emissions rose by 15% between 1975 and 1985.

The damage to trees by acid rain can, of course, lead to the build-up of carbon dioxide and the greenhouse effect. Damage has occurred in over half the West German forests and in extensive areas of Switzerland, Austria, Poland, Yugoslavia and the Netherlands. In an unpublished report, the Czechoslovakian Academy of Sciences estimated that 37% of the country's forests were already dead or irreparably damaged and that this would be increased to 60% by the year 2000 unless pollution is reduced. Assistant Professor Bengt Nihlgard of the University of Lund, Sweden, visited several woods in England and commented *'the only place where I have seen correspondingly bad situations in central Europe before is around the biggest airports in West Germany'*.

Rainforests

Friends of the Earth have estimated that deforestation has contributed 25% of the total release of carbon dioxide into the environment. To date, 12% of the Brazilian rainforests have been destroyed. This destruction is being carried out for a number of reasons; to support the export of hardwoods, for fuel, and to clear land for subsistence agriculture. More than 60% of tropical hardwoods come from just six countries and half the exported wood goes to Japan. Much of the recent loss of the Central American rainforest has been for beef production to meet the demand of the fast food market in the United States.

In May 1989, eight countries of the Amazon basin — Brazil, Colombia, Ecuador, Guyana, Peru, Surinam, Bolivia and Venezuela — met in the heart of Brazil's rainforest. They issued an 'Amazon Declaration' in which they urged rich countries to provide money for the preservation of the world's greatest rainforest. They also criticised the $400 billion foreign debt which they said was impossible to pay under present conditions. In addition, several heads of state criticised the harm done to the environment by the developed countries.

So in conclusion we can see that national income statistics do not directly measure the problems of pollution and there are many ways in which reductions in production would lead to a cleaner and more healthy environment for all.

CRIME PREVENTION MEASURES COUNT AS WEALTH

If the fear of crime increases, then there will be more and more security locks, safes and alarms. A London security leaflet advertised the fact that one in five buildings are burgled each year and that glass is broken in less than fifty per cent of cases. It outlined a range of security devices available such as window locks, door viewers and chains and, for those who leave nothing to chance, the 'invincible mortice locks'. If burglary increases, these firms will then be able to advertise that one in four or even one in three buildings are burgled each year and sales of preventative methods may well grow beyond expectations.

There was a spate of burglaries in Long Island a few years ago which prompted the local companies to promote the sales of alarms. Many people decided to install them at great expense, linked to the local police station. This has caused the police great inconvenience as they are often accidentally activated which is a waste of police time. Similarly, car thefts have led to the fitting of alarms. A Brooklyn resident told me that these things were not only expensive but also caused a great deal of inconvenience. Very often the car is parked in another street which means the alarm cannot be heard by the owner. Many people are woken in the middle of the night by an alarm that has been set off by vibration. So an increase in fear leading to burglary protection is a waste of resources and can also lead to negative side effects. It is also sad that in recent years we have seen increased sales of anti-rape devices such as sprays or alarms. My mother remembers when she went to the station in the middle of the night during the war so my father could get the last train possible to arrive back at his ship on time. She walked the three miles back home at two or three in the morning without a thought of being attacked. That could not happen these days. Indeed, if any woman were to go out alone, be attacked and report it to the police, there is little doubt she would be criticised for being foolhardy.

In most, if not all, countries of the developed world there have been large increases in the number of crimes. In Britain between 1971 and 1988, the number of thefts more than doubled and the level of violence against the person increased two and a half times. The number of people applying for legal aid because of criminal proceedings doubled. These changes also will look good in terms of the measurement of GNP. One of the major points this book makes is that we should be creating a new kind of attitude towards material goods and our interpersonal relationships which would remove the desire to steal and make it safe to walk the streets. People should want to spend their time constructively — helping others rather than wanting to assault, rob and steal.

LITIGATION FEVER

An increase in use of the law will lead to an increase in measured services but not necessarily to the benefit of society. In Britain, between 1971 and 1988, the number of divorces went up more than six times. Some of this rise was due to changes in the law which meant that people could regularise their marital situation. As there are usually problems to be sorted out with marital breakdown, the lawyers' fees for contested divorces will count as positive in the measured wealth but negative for many in the sum total of human happiness.

Chapter Four will consider the fact that much surgery carried out is unnecessary, partly due to the fear of litigation. Several doctors told me that in the United States, one of the reasons for the increase in surgery was that when no-fault compensation was introduced for car crashes, the lawyers lost an important source of their income. They considered other ways of making money and hit upon medicine. So doctors are now carrying out many tests for which there is no real need, just to cover themselves with 'defensive medicine'. Of course they make money, so the patient suffers by having treatment which is both unpleasant and more expensive. Unnecessary surgery is much less common in Britain but has been increasing.

So in general, an increase in crime or legal intervention will count as positive in terms of growth but will probably reflect as negative in terms of the quality of life.

OUR SELFISH WANTS CAN DAMAGE OTHERS

Quite apart from the question of pollution, sometimes an individual's wants may conflict with those of society. Transport is a good subject to illustrate some points in this respect. One would hope for a steady improvement which would allow all sections of society to enjoy cheap, easy and pleasant travel. However, this has not happened in reality.

All Western European countries have subsidised public transport. However, the balance in Britain and the United States between the car and public transport has been tilted towards the car. This is evident, for example, in the heavy investment in road building. However it is possible to have a totally different philosophy which would give priority to public transport, with the private car being supplementary.

Some economists are totally opposed to cars. Mishan, for example, has said that *the private automobile is, surely, one of the greatest, if not the greatest, disasters that ever befell the human race*. He asserted that almost every principle of architectural harmony has been perverted in the struggle to keep the mounting volume of motorised traffic moving. He rightly argued that the volume of traffic is such that clamour, dust, fumes, congestion and visual distraction are the predominant features in all built-up areas whether it is London, New York, Birmingham, Chicago, Paris, Tokyo, Dusseldorf or Milan. Nowadays people are faced with traffic instead of the mingling of the crowds and the enjoyment of the gaiety associated with the great cities of the past.

Few will go as far as agreeing with Mishan that the motor car is the greatest disaster known to mankind, however it is possible to see great advantages in public transport being given priority and having cars in a back-up role to be used primarily for special groups. One of the great frustrations of modern society is the fact that many people spend a great deal of their lives stuck in traffic jams. This is both a tremendous waste of time and of precious resources. In 1989 reports of the costs of traffic congestion came out from London and Delhi. In Delhi it was calculated that 20% of the fuel used is wasted. In London, the Confederation of British Industry (CBI) reported that the cost of transport congestion was £15 billion a year — five times higher than previously calculated and costs each household at least five pounds a week. The CBI also recognised the effect of the congestion in increasing working days lost through hypertension, heart disease and neuroses, much of it due to the stress of getting to and from work.

It is a strange lack of planning that leads to so many spending their lives sitting in cars, isolated from other people and arriving at their destination tired and frustrated. The changes to improve society cannot be brought about by market forces because this is one of many areas where they do not work effectively. This can clearly be seen by an example.

Imagine a group of people in a village going to work at a local factory ten miles away. At first, the journey takes half an hour, including the time taken to walk to the bus and waiting for it. Some people realise that if they go by car they can get to the factory in a quarter of an hour. It is more expensive, but they save time. By the time half the group are travelling by car, there are traffic jams. The time to travel to work by car is now half an hour. So there is no improvement over the first situation and the drivers have to continue spending the extra money and have less social contact. Those travelling by bus are much worse off because while they wait for the bus, they have to breathe in car fumes. Their journey time may now be an hour as the bus has to travel through the jams and comes less frequently than before. In all there will have been a great increase in measured wealth, but for many, a reduction in the quality of life.

The people who drive cars are predominantly the fittest adults. The elderly and children have least access, yet these are the groups who are likely to have most problems in walking to public transport.

The advantages of promoting public transport are many, but some of the important points are as follows:

- The overall death rates of society would be reduced because public transport is much safer than the car.

- There would be fewer fumes and less noise. This would lead to an increase in children's intelligence because the effects of leaded petrol would be reduced.

- There would be a greater sense of community as people would meet each other either walking towards the transport or travelling on it.

- There is likely to be less crime as the greater number of people on the streets would give added protection to vulnerable groups.

- The danger from cars and the paucity of public transport means that many parents cannot leave their children to travel on their own. Parents are forever picking up and ferrying rather than allowing their children independence of travel.

- Passengers on public transport are able to engage in cultural activities while travelling. They can read books and newspapers, and even prepare reports or write lectures. With initiative, travel can become carefree and very much a positive part of life.

So in all a more community-based system of transport could greatly improve social life and the environment.

DESTROY A THEATRE TO MAKE A MILLION

All countries have a stock of buildings which are part of their heritage. The use of these buildings is free to the community except for the cost of running repairs and the stock of houses cannot be changed very much from year to year. If a political decision were taken to remove the preservation orders on many buildings to allow the construction of office blocks, it is likely that there would be a spurious increase in growth. The loss of the free benefit to everyone would not be counted. Measured wealth would be created as profits accrued for the demolition and construction companies. High rents could be charged for the office space.

There are often debates about the London theatres and whether they should be destroyed to make way for office blocks which would give a more 'realistic' return on investment. If the theatre were knocked down, there would be the loss of a live venue and consequently a reduction in the cultural life of the community. The measured wealth would increase as greater profits accrued to surveyors, architects and building companies. The community does, however, have to bear in mind the potential losses in terms of cultural development, aesthetic appeal and longer term economic factors. Many people have had great sympathy with the criticisms made by Prince Charles. On 1 December 1987 he accused Britain's architects of doing more damage than Adolf Hitler's Luftwaffe. He followed this with a television documentary in October 1988 in which he called the National Theatre 'A nuclear power station in the middle of London' and the Convention Centre at Birmingham 'an unmitigated disaster.' The architects defended themselves when, in April 1989, the Prince highlighted the threat to historic towns from ugly housing developments. Marcus Binney of Save Britain's Heritage, welcomed his support. Binney argued that because the Government had so relaxed planning controls in the late 1980's, a building boom was leading to environmental destruction.

Too many architects have built houses unsuitable for the people who have to live in them. When designing estates they should position the buildings so the children can play outside with the buildings surrounding them. The youngsters will then be safe from traffic and parents can keep an eye on them. Planners should also ensure that games such as football and cricket are catered for in play areas. A sign on a local estate says *No Ball Games Allowed* and predictably the children have painted out the word 'No' and play football in whatever little space left to them. They face unnecessary danger because they are playing amidst the concrete walls and holes the architects have littered around.

Countries have other natural factors such as good weather or natural beauty. Those which are warmer can probably survive with less measured wealth then cooler countries. In Britain and the USA, if the winter is mild then it leads to less fuel consumption for heat and a reduction in measured wealth from this part of the economy. Gloves and scarves have fewer sales as do snow boots, sledges and snow ploughs. Similarly, a hot summer's day may lead to people walking rather than taking their cars, to less clothing being worn and to a decline in the takings of venues with indoor entertainment. These effects may well offset the increase in sales of soft drinks, summer clothes and sunglasses and overall the measured wealth might decrease.

QUALITY OF LIFE NOT QUANTITY OF GOODS

The final point is important and it concerns the kind of society we wish to create. It could be that to achieve a high rate of growth we have to work harder, or for longer hours or do more tedious jobs. If this happens, the wealth will have been bought at a cost and possibly too high a cost.

Sociologists have noted that people's jobs affect their social life and limit the kinds of activities in which they can engage. Anyone who has a physically demanding job knows that in the evenings, there is little energy to pursue any cultural activity that calls for a great deal of effort. Also some non-manual occupations tend to create tension which can disrupt family life. One study showed company directors to have a divorce rate nearly three times the national average. One possible problem is that the business world limits responsibility and authority, judges people for what they can do rather than for what they are and sometimes rewards aggressiveness. These are not values likely to lead to a successful family life. So a movement towards a more thrusting and aggressive society may increase measured wealth but lead to people developing the kind of personality which will be harmful to relationships.

British newscasters for the radio programme 'Today' travelling to Japan, found businessmen who were spending only a few minutes each day with their children. They were often expected to spend most evenings in work-related social gatherings without their spouses. Studies of occupations in Britain and the United States have also shown conflicts with family life and care of children. On the other hand, in recent years, many people have decided to reduce their income in order to have a lifestyle which allows them to spend time with their family. A young businessman importing shoes from Spain 'had' to go on a business trip at the time his second child was due and so he missed his daughter's birth. He decided he was giving up too much in the pursuit of his career. So he gave up his high-powered job and moved to the country where he felt he could be a much better parent. If others in society took similar decisions, the measured wealth might be reduced but the quality of their lives would be enhanced.

Others have not taken such drastic action, but have made sure that they take time out of a busy week to pick their children up from school and spend time with them, despite the possible cost in terms of their career or business.

There are times when individuals or societies need to sit back and ask what they are doing with their lives. It is too easy to be swept along by economic success and the pursuit of wealth. This applies in particular to countries which are the economic success stories. To return to Japan as an example. The country has made great progress in selling its equipment around the world. However, it might be sensible for the people to ask whether such a high percentage of the population need to spend their lives making cars, videos, television sets, radios and cameras for the rest of the world. Countries should ask, not what will make us the most money, but what is the best way forward in helping people to develop their social and personal relationships and improve the quality of their lives.

It is clear that, especially in the developed countries, economic growth is a very poor indicator of the quality of life. There are many ways that an increase in measured wealth can have a negative effect. What we should be considering is the changes that can be made to improve our use of time rather than how society can produce more goods. The next chapter suggests a different perspective on the economy.

Chapter 3

Enough is Enough

In the first two chapters I showed the poor correlation between wealth and the quality of life and gave a number of reasons why this might be the case. In this chapter, I argue that we should be concentrating on the quality of goods produced. While there is a case for an increase in production in certain areas, overall, the developed countries should not be aiming for further growth. Although some areas of the economy should maintain their growth, other areas should remain at an optimum level while some should be reduced. This approach can lead to improvements in the quality of life without conflicting with the environment. It can also help to free us from the treadmill of thinking in terms of ever-increasing wants, and life as one great competition where there are winners and losers with wealth being the criteria for victory. This chapter draws out some of the implications of this approach.

AREAS OF INCREASED PRODUCTION

When we talk about increasing production, this is linked to two main areas of concern. The first is the failure of the society to provide the basics of life to many groups. The second depends upon the kind of society we wish to create.

The examples in the Introduction indicate that in the deprived areas of the world, there is a need to increase production of necessities such as food, clothing and shelter. In Chapter Six on world poverty, techniques are discussed which will not only improve people's lives but also enhance the environment. In addition there should be universal provision of clean water, adequate food and health care for all sections of society and homes for everyone.

Another important point is that studies show many people do not have access to the birth control techniques they desire. Provision of these will enable people to only have the number of children they want.

In the richer nations, we need to help people who, for various reasons, are deprived of the wealth in which others share. One particular area where there are great shortages at the moment is in the help given to parents. The early years of child rearing can lead to great poverty for many couples. In the majority of cases, the woman gives up her job. The man may have to work overtime to make up the deficiency in income which leaves him very little time to take a full role in child rearing. As an illustration of the problems that families can face, I became friendly with a garage owner at my swimming club. We chatted and he told me that he liked to take time out of his day, a period of relaxation away from the cares of his job. He also told me how he organised his life in order that he could spend time with his children. Apart from seeing them at weekends, he often took them to school. Although he usually worked until 6.30 or 7.00pm, at least one day a week he met his children from school and took them to the park. We got on quite well together and I performed my clown act at his daughter's birthday party. However, an opportunity arose for him to take on a second garage which he felt would provide him with a pension. When this opened he more or less disappeared from the club, and the added responsibility meant that he spent less time with his children, and he missed out on much of their development. In this case there was an element of choice, but many people are forced by their adverse financial situation to work excessively long hours when their children are young. So a transfer of resources towards helping the family is something that would be conducive to improving the quality of life.

When talking about increasing production, the question as to the kind of society we wish to create is important. I would like to see a change towards returnable and recyclable items at the expense of those that contribute to the waste problem. So I would like to see the promotion of light bulbs that last for many years, razor blades that do not have to be disposed of so often, toughened crockery which will not break or chip at the slightest accident, and batteries that are rechargeable rather than just used for a short while and then thrown away adding to the volume of waste.

I would like a move away from passive entertainment such as television and towards more active pursuits. I would like more goods produced that would encourage people to be productive in their social life, eg. pianos, guitars, balls, cricket sets, tennis rackets, squash balls 55 and equipment, running shorts and shoes, aerobic equipment, football boots etc.

One very noticeable change in Britain in recent years is the decline of park facilities. I would like to see local architects consulting local children and parents to provide facilities which allow a variety of activities and at the same time improve the environment.

Children, in general, should be playing more sports and games. So I would like to see increased sales of stilts, marbles, spinning tops, diabolos, yo yo's and other similar items.

Currently very few adults take part in leisure pursuits such as painting, writing poetry etc. More services and goods should be made available to encourage people to be more creative.

As already mentioned, health care in Britain is suffering shortages. Expenditure on health has been much below that of comparable countries. People are dying unnecessarily due to shortages of necessary equipment such as kidney machines. The cutbacks in hospital beds due to cash constraints have also led to great delays in health care especially for non-urgent operations. We do have choices in how we spend our money and a first priority should be to provide people with good health care at the time they become ill. It should also be free from money worries and bureaucratic interference.

I would like to see more done for the elderly and they in turn to be encouraged to do more for society. There should be a change in the economic structure to enable old people to buy things they need in sufficient quantities, and in particular to protect against such dangers as hypothermia. There should also be a recognition of the fact that the able-bodied elderly have much to offer to the younger generation. They could be more involved in helping in schools on a volunteer basis, teaching children how to read, for example.

I would like to see many more cycles on the roads and special cycle lanes to prevent accidents. This is discussed more fully when considering energy later in this chapter.

AREAS OF OPTIMUM PRODUCTION

There are many areas of life where if our needs are met we should not need more. In this section I consider three crucial areas — food production, transport and energy.

a) Food production

Currently on a worldwide basis, food production is unevenly distributed. In the United States, a quarter of the population is overweight and in Europe there are good surpluses with farmers being paid to cut production. Yet still the food is adulterated and diets are generally less healthy than they should be. In contrast, in other parts of the world there are food shortages and children suffering brain damage from malnutrition. So any moves to improve the quality and distribution of food are to be welcomed.

On the first of January 1989, the Common Market banned American meat. This was because animals in the United States were given growth hormones which left residues which the Common Market argued were unnecessary and could be dangerous to health. Many animals are given female hormones to encourage growth and these can then be passed down the food chain. One British woman commentator advised at the time of the US prohibition 'Do we want to risk all our young men growing boobs?'. This feeding of animals with growth drugs is clearly a dubious practice for it is purely profit oriented without any thought to the future health problems. The vast majority of the American population find it impossible to buy meat which is naturally produced, even if they are prepared to pay a higher price for drug-free meat. Apart from drugs, we also know that animals raised under intensive farming methods are more likely to have saturated rather than unsaturated fat which increases the chances of heart attacks.

In general, the subject of food is one area where it is much more sensible to consider an optimum. Once the food level has increased to around 3,000 calories per person, per day, it is crucial to have the best balanced diet with the lowest number of harmful additives.

In fact in Britain, the Royal Society of Medicine in January 1989, argued that wholesale dietary change is necessary to reduce the number of 180,000 people who die of heart disease each year. In 1984, the medical authorities produced a report recommending that the proportion of food energy provided by fat should be reduced to a maximum of 35%, but in fact it remained constant at 42%. Professor Philip James, one of the authors of the 1989 report, said that *'Senior medical officers in Europe seem to regard the British experience as either a total disaster or as a control group against which to measure progress in the rest of Europe'*. Another of the authors, Professor Gerald Shaper, pointed out that 60% of British middle-aged men doubled their risks of heart attack by their blood cholesterol level alone, despite the fact that a reduction in fat consumption could dramatically lower it. In September 1989 *The Lancet* published research showing that eating oily fish helped to reduce the chances of a heart attack.

In the USA, the Surgeon General produced a report on nutrition and health in July 1988 based on the data from more than 2,500 scientific studies which, officials hoped, would eventually have as much influence as the 1964 Surgeon General's report on smoking. It had a clear warning that Americans should reduce their intake of fats in order to lead healthier lives. It notes that saturated fats are a major contribution to high blood cholesterol levels which can lead to coronary heart disease. Nutritionists interviewed said that red meats and dairy products are prime sources of saturated fats. Popular foods in this category include hamburgers and processed meats such as hot dogs, pork and ham, ice cream, butter, whole milk and fast foods deep fried in lard or beef fat. Some plants such as palm kernel oil and coconut oil also contain saturated fat. The report suggested that Americans should eat more vegetables, fruits, whole grain foods, fish, poultry, lean meats and low fat dairy products. The American Heart Association noted that Americans obtain an average 37% of their calories from fat and has set a goal of not more than 30% of fat in the diet. This is 5% below the British target and furthermore Dr Michael McGinnis, a deputy assistant secretary for health, said that a future fat standard might be 'well below that (30%) target' (*Newsday* 2 August 1988).

In a book entitled *Elite Deviance,* Simon and Eitzen considered the impact of television advertising on children's eating habits. Advertising to children is a billion dollar industry. They stressed that the nutritional problem is that the most commonly advertised food products are sugar coated cereals, candies and other sweet snack foods. One study showed that of youngsters in grades one to five, 75% had asked their mothers to buy cereals they had seen on television. Another study showed that 96% of all food advertising on Saturday and Sunday children's TV programs was for sweets. The report by the Federal Trade Commission found that parents often purchased foods requested by their children — to list acceptable snacks, children named cookies, candy, cake and ice cream including specific heavily-advertised products.

The authors continued to argue that television directed at children is effective because advertisers have done their research. Motivational research has been used to analyse the way children respond to different stimuli.

In 1978, the Federal Trade Commission proposed that all television commercials aimed at children under the age of eight were basically unfair and should be banned, as should adverts for all highly sugared products for children under the age of eleven. The spokesman for Kelloggs argued that people must care for themselves and the last thing needed was a national nanny. In Britain too, advertisers encourage children to learn dietary habits which, if continued into adulthood, will lead to problems of consumption of excess sugar, dental caries, obesity and an increased chance of diabetes.

Food pollution — how much is hidden from us?

The pressure of the market can also lead to possible side effects. One of the big changes in animal production is in the longevity of chickens' lives. When I was a child we used to buy baby chicks and fatten them up for Christmas. In the early Seventies, during a discussion with a farmer's daughter about their chickens, she told me that they had managed to reduce the lives of the cocks to twelve weeks by injecting them with female hormones at one week and eight weeks. She was expecting to get this down further to nine weeks by means of other drugs. Nowadays, the average length of life is only seven weeks. However, I have my doubts about the effects of these drugs on the consumer. To examine the effects properly would involve a large-scale study lasting about twenty years but this is clearly not about to be undertaken.

THE PEST OF PESTICIDES

Even vegetarians are not immune from possible problems of pollution of food. According to the environmental group 'Friends of the Earth', vegetables in the Midlands had cadmium levels ten times the maximum permitted, (*The Observer* 11 March 1984). An advertisement for the car firm Volkswagen advertising lead-free petrol, stated that levels of lead in cabbage and lettuce were ten times as high as those in peas because they are cushioned against pollution by their pods.

Friends of the Earth point out that pesticides are used in the production of 97% of the fruit, vegetables and cereals we eat. A 1987 briefing sheet stated that pesticides are chemicals designed to kill organisms that we think are either a threat to our well-being or will destroy crops. Herbicides are used to kill weeds, fungicides to control plant diseases and insecticides to destroy the insects which threaten crops. However, most pesticides not only kill unwanted plants and insects but they are also toxic to humans — some are so poisonous that less than one teaspoonful will kill an adult. A few drops of the herbicide paraquat, in its undiluted form, can be fatal. The adverse effects of pesticides to humans can be divided into two categories. Acute effects which occur immediately — these include nausea, giddiness, and even unconsciousness, and those effects which become evident after a period of time — the chronic effects. These include cancer, tumour formation and birth defects. A study by the National Academy of Sciences in the USA in 1987 showed that 90% (by weight) of fungicides used in America have some tumour forming capability. Another American study showed that of fifty commonly used non-agricultural pesticides, only one had actually been tested for its chronic effects to the degree required by US law. The other 49 are still under suspicion, (General Accounting Office 1986). In Britain, some pesticides continue to be used despite being banned in other countries and others are doubtful because they were tested over ten years ago. *59*

These were not subject to the safety reviews which, for the 300 pesticides used in the UK could take 20 years. In fact, two which were re-tested — dinoseb and cyhexatin — have been banned under suspicion of causing birth defects. When tests were carried out to find pesticide residues in glasshouse grown lettuces by the British Ministry of Agriculture, it was discovered that they could vary by a factor of between 5 and 100. One of the pesticides found was dimethoate which, as the Environmental Protection Agency in the USA found, possesses risks of mutagenic, reproductive and foetotoxic effects.

At present there is no way that the British consumer can tell if pesticides have been used in food, despite the fact that a survey conducted by Friends of the Earth in 1985 found that 85% of the population would be prepared to pay more for food that was pesticide free. The organisation also said that although food production would drop by between 25% and 40% if all pesticides were banned, it is possible to produce enough good crops with many fewer pesticides than at present.

FACTORY FARMING

Factory farming has problems which are two-fold, it produces inferior food and also brings unnecessary suffering to animals. In Britain, the organisation 'Compassion in World Farming' (20 Lavant Street, Petersfield, Hampshire) has produced numerous reports on the subject. One is entitled *Eating the cruelty-free way* and argues that while Compassion in World Farming does not tell people how they should live, what they should wear, eat or do, it does ask people to take the trouble to find out how food is produced and what the cost may be in terms of animal suffering. Its message is 'Don't buy your food in ignorance'. It argues that factory farming methods involve deprivation and imprisonment for animals but that if people are given information about the lives of the food animals, they then have a choice. They may say they don't care and want to go on eating factory farmed produce and reject the whole idea of a cruelty-free diet. Or they may decide to continue eating meat and eggs bought only from free-range farms where the animals have a better quality of life. Free-range eggs are now stocked by an increasing number of shops and supermarket chains, as well as health food stores. Some butchers and supermarkets are also stocking free-range meat or 'humanely pro-duced meat'. One important point the organisation makes is that a cruelty-free diet is also a healthy diet. That apart from reduction in fat, experts also recommend an increased intake of fibre, found in veget-ables, fruit and whole grain cereals. So by following these guidelines, and keeping sugar and salt intakes low, people should be well on the way to a healthier lifestyle, as well as a more compassionate one.

In addition, the organisation notes that some people feel that slaughter itself constitutes cruelty, and so want to follow a vegetarian or vegan diet.

Compassion in World Farming has also set out the advantages of free-range animals over those factory farmed as follows:

FREE-RANGE ANIMALS

- Mean grassland, hedges and rotational farming.
- Eat mostly rough fodders unsuited for human consumption.
- Can utilize land that is difficult to cultivate
- Recycle their wastes into renewed soil fertility.
- Maintain their health with the minimum use of drugs.
- Through their active self expression, they make a valuable contribution to the countryside scene.

FACTORY FARM ANIMALS

- Compete directly with people for food, consume oilseed proteins needed in the countries where they are grown in the fight against malnutrition.
- Create the need for continuous corn growing, which in turn calls for more chemical fertilisers, weed killers and pesticides, to the detriment of the wildlife of the countryside.
- Waste primary food (only 10% efficiency).
- Cause air and water pollution.
- Degrade the sensibilities of all who work with them.
- Threaten your health because of the drug residues and pathogens which they pass on in their products and meat.

Lord Mackie in the House of Lords put his view of the battery system. He said that as a farmer he detested it. For, although it produces cheap eggs, free-range ones would certainly be worth half as much again as eggs produced in a battery. He hoped the Government would work towards getting batteries abolished throughout the European Community. People would then have better quality eggs to eat and hens would take up some of the land that is currently used to produce surplus food. So there would be benefits all round.

As a sign of the increasing concern, in 1988 the Archbishop of Canterbury announced the formation of a Church of England Commission on Rural Affairs, chaired by a former Minister of Agriculture, to look at life in rural areas. This was welcomed by Clive Hollands, Secretary of the St Andrew Animal Fund, who said that the overproduction of food whilst half the world starves, and the plight of animals reared in intensive husbandry systems, are matters of vital importance. He saw the appointment of the Commission as a development to be welcomed by all thinking Christians as a first step in preventing further damage and waste, and above all, in granting animals reared for food the right to a good life and a quiet death.

Another important move occurred in 1988. Sweden banned factory farming stating that animal rearing will be geared towards keeping animals healthy and happy. Under the new law, battery hen rearing will be phased out by 1998, farmers will be obliged to graze cows outside and provide pigs with roomier and more pleasant sties. The permanent tethering of pigs is banned and the law calls for the animals to have separate places to sleep, rest and feed.

So there have been some important changes. The main organisations, including Compassion in World Farming, have been specifically concerned with the treatment of a number of animals. I shall briefly outline some of the main points they make.

CHICKENS

In 1979 the Frankfurt High Court decided that keeping hens in battery cages which did not allow them to exercise their inherited behaviour pattern, was an offence under German law. It seems such a change would be popular in Britain. An opinion poll in 1983 showed only 13% found the battery hen acceptable. Eighty-two per cent agreed that if cages continued to be used, they should be big enough for the hens to stretch out their wings. They would need to be five times the present size. Currently in cages there are no nest boxes, no perches, no solid floor and no bedding to scratch in. The wingspan of a chicken is 30-32" yet five birds are kept in a cage only 20" wide. To the argument that the hens would not lay if they weren't happy, the answer is that every committee that has considered this idea has rejected it. Chickens are reared in such a way that they have to lay eggs whether they like it or not.

On the subject of producing chickens for the table, in the United Kingdom about 500 million chickens are intensively reared in huge windowless sheds. Unlike battery hens, they are not in cages, but live loose on the floor on woodshavings. A leaflet *Consumer Alert* states *'Rats and flies thrive around broiler farms, and maggots have been seen breeding on birds with open wounds. It's not surprising that 20-30 million birds die annually in their sheds, before reaching slaughter age. A broiler house worker describes collecting the dead birds. "This has to be done every day because of the heat and the way the birds are tightly packed together. When you pick up a dead bird it is quite common for them to be so putrid that they are just bags of bone and fluid." Chicken pieces on sale (legs and wings) will often have been removed from injured or diseased birds, at the processing stage.'*

At the end of 1988 there was a great deal of controversy in Britain about salmonella incidence in eggs and chickens. This led to sales of eggs plummeting and the Government paying out over five million pounds in compensation to the producers. Dr B Rowe, Director of the British Central Public Health Laboratory commented: *'The high incidence of salmonella infection in broiler chickens is certainly partially due to the intensive rearing system.'* Compassion for World farming recommends people write for a list of suppliers of free-range chickens and a copy of their cruelty-free diet sheet.

COWS

There has been a British campaign to stop the licensing of BST, the genetically-engineered growth hormone now being experimentally injected into cattle to increase milk yield. Professor John Webster of Bristol University commented that we are not so poverty-stricken as a society that we need to stick needles in cows to get more milk. He is right to be concerned, for two thirds of the nine early trials in the United States suggest adverse reactions to the drugs. However, even if the drugs can be made to work, is it a good thing to unnecessarily interfere with nature? If we started to use the drug in 1991 we would have to wait until the year 2001 before the effects of the drug after ten years are known.

Other issues in which Compassion in World Farming has been involved include the cruel killing of frogs for their legs. It achieved success when this was banned in India. It has also opposed the force feeding of ducks in France and the keeping of calves in poor conditions for veal production.

Almost every day during the course of writing this book there has been some form of media concern about the safety of foods. As I write today, for example, there is a report that the US government has banned an insecticide, which is used on one in twenty British apples, and which is absorbed by the fruit and is suspected of causing cancer.

Given the fact that there is such a food surplus in the rich countries, there is a good case for food to be produced as naturally as possible.

TRANSPORT

The conflict between private and public transport was brought to public notice in Britain with a front page report in *The Times* (5 Dec. 1988) entitled 'When traffic jams determine life and death.' The report quoted one of Britain's leading experts on traffic flow as saying that 31 people may well not have died in the King's Cross disaster if fire   *63* engines had been able to reach the tube station more quickly. He told *The Times* that loss of life might have been prevented if measures had been taken to allow proper movement of emergency vehicles through the capital. If the firefighters had arrived in time they could well have controlled the flames along an escalator before they produced a 'flashover' in the station's ticket hall. This occurred two minutes after the fire engine arrived. Its speed on the journey had been only 7 mph. One expert, Dr Mogridge of London University, called for a shift of current road space from the car to the bus or the tram, so that they can run on a segregated track. This could then easily be made available for emergency services and fire, police and ambulances would be guaranteed a fast route avoiding congestion. It is ironical that it is only a minority who travel by car. Of those who travel to central London, two in five (40%) arrive by rail, over a third (36%) arrive by tube and 7% arrive by bus. Only one in seven (14%) of commuters arrive by car. So the traffic jams are largely caused by a small minority.

Mogridge has carried out research which is important not only to London but also to the other major cities. After interviews with 300,000 Londoners, he suggests that in a busy road system where there are alternative routes between two points, motorists will swap between them until the average journey time becomes the same on each. *The Times* report suggested it was rather like water flowing through various channels and finding the same level in each. Mogridge also suggested that the same principle applies to door-to-door journey times whether by car or public transport. If road is quicker, people will switch to it until the route becomes so congested that there is no longer an advantage.

This research ties in with the point I made in discussing the problems of economic growth. If people begin to move away from public transport to cars, the actual journey time on both becomes longer. The only solution therefore is to improve public transport. The market by itself will not solve the problem. In London, the roads are often clogged up by cars and on an average journey in central London the car will be stationary for almost a third of the time. In the evening rush hour in 1968, the average speed was twelve and a half miles an hour. Despite many attempts to improve the roads, by 1986 this had fallen to eleven and a half. The only time there was a noticeable improvement was in 1974 when the oil crisis drove up petrol prices and traffic speed went up to a heady 14 miles an hour.

The transport system can only achieve true efficiency if a substantial number of car drivers switch to public transport. This will help to increase the revenue needed to improve the service for both former drivers and existing passengers and also will leave the roads free for essential services and freight. In addition, it will improve the health of society as private transport leads to more deaths on the roads.

The Japanese experience illustrates the problems that private transport can cause at a national level. From 1970 Japan's wealth grew until it reached the level of income of the United States which had hitherto been the richest major country in the world. The number of cars increased from 6.7 million to 26.7 million and the number of miles passengers were carried by cars more than doubled. The length of roads increased by only 11% so it is not difficult to see why Japan's increasing wealth has led to a great deal of congestion. The number of bus passengers declined during the sixteen years from 12 million to eight and a half million and rail transport also declined. In 1970 Japan's railways performed the carriage of almost half (49%) of the passenger miles. By 1986 it had declined to 38%. It is not surprising that we hear so many stories of Japanese road congestion and many other countries face the same fate.

Introducing a further point, Irving Mintzer of World Resources Institute, a private research group in Washington, argued that global warming would be reduced by mass (public) transport, without much sacrifice of American living standards. He argued for an increase in gas excise tax to $1 a gallon, combined with penalties against owners of 'gas guzzlers' which would be paid to drivers of new efficient cars. He did, however, recognise that the measure would be politically impossible at the present time.

PRO-BIKE POLICIES

There are a number of good reasons for the promotion of cycling — both to society and the individual. Andy Clarke has made a number of points. Cycling does not pollute the air in contrast to the damage to health caused by car fumes nor does it consume the world's precious fossil fuels. A majority study by the US government in 1980 found that a realistic five year plan to increase cycling by 500% would result in annual savings of between 16 and 23 million barrels of oil. Cycling will also eliminate traffic jams because bicycles need much less space than cars. A four metre wide cycle path will carry five times as many people as a road twice as wide.

Two out of five households do not have access to a car, yet planners act as if access is universal. Provision for cyclists will reduce the number of deaths from road accidents and will also improve the nation's health. Cycling is one of the best all-round forms of exercise and may be seen as a form of preventive medicine. At the moment, government policies have not promoted cycling and the roads are very dangerous. Many children who could cycle to school are ferried by their parents because there are inadequate cycle paths. In 1984/5 the British Department of Transport allocated £3,000 million to roads and only one quarter of a million pounds to cycle facilities. This is despite the fact that, as the Chief Engineer of Stevenage Development Corporation commented, *'Cycle paths give you motorways for the price of footpaths'*. At the moment, cyclists are about seventeen times as more vulnerable on the road as car drivers, yet they rarely cause others serious damage. The lack of finance for adequate cycle tracks is a major cause of this risk. Other countries have taken a different approach. The Dutch Ministry of Transport is engaged in a major programme to provide facilities for cyclists and about 30% of trips in urban areas are made by bicycle. In Denmark, a survey taken on 10th October 1983, revealed that 41% of people cycled to work. So a change in policy by the governments of other developed countries could well have marked effects on the safety of cyclists, and in turn, the health and mobility of the community.

To sum up, this section has shown that the best transport system is not produced by the individuals in the society pursuing their own interests. The social policy towards transport needs to account for the interest of all sections of the community.

ENERGY

The current world policy on energy cannot be sustained in the long term as we are rapidly using up fossil fuels. In many ways, the world is fortunate in that it is relatively well blessed. However, as mentioned in the Introduction, if every country consumed oil at the rate of the United States, then known reserves would be rapidly depleted. There are, of course, more coal and gas reserves which will last for several hundred years. However, the limits on energy are such that it is clear that not every country is going to be able to consume it at the same rate as that of the United States. Also, in future years I suspect people will be shocked by the speed with which Britain used up its North Sea oil. In fact the rich countries are in the process of a once-and-for-all stripping of the world of its sources of cheap fuel. A few years ago I spoke to an old schoolfriend who emigrated to the United States and went to work in Indonesia for an oil company. On returning on vacation, he told me that the United States could produce enough of its own oil if it wanted to but 'it was better to use up the Indonesians' oil first'. The world proven reserves of oil are about 650 billion barrels and there may be large new discoveries. Annual consumption is down to about seven eighths of its peak in 1979, and may well be reduced further as people move to more energy-efficient cars and hopefully change their lifestyles towards public transport. However, it is likely that, unless great changes are made, the world supplies of oil will be severely depleted in thirty years time even if the developing countries do not significantly increase their consumption.

Coal is the fossil fuel with the greatest projected reserves. In Britain it is estimated it will last for two or three hundred years depending on new finds and levels of consumption. It does, of course, create a number of problems, however. One of the most important being acid rain.

The other fossil fuels include natural gas, oil shale and tar sands. At the moment, countries like the United States obtain about nine tenths of their primary energy requirements from fossil fuels. This will have to change in the long term, and the world's energy supplies will have to come from renewable energy sources or from nuclear power with all its associated problems. In the United States the nuclear power industry has proved to be unacceptable. On 28 March 1979, less than a year after it had opened, the Three Mile Island nuclear accident led to a hydrogen explosion and more than 20 tons of molten fuel at temperatures of more than 5,000 degrees Fahrenheit crashing down. The clean-up has, so far, cost $1.000 million which is $300 million more than the plant cost to build. The result has been that all the 47 plants ordered in the five years up to the accident were cancelled and no new nuclear plant has been ordered since.

An as yet unsolved problem is that of how to dispose of reactors after they have served their usefulness. One idea was to cloak them in concrete, and after about thirty years hope that their radiation would have reduced to safe levels. However, some of the radioactive sources have half lives — the time when the level of radiation would have halved from its original level — much longer than earlier thought. One has a half life of 20,300 years and another 80,000 years. So, long after the concrete tomb had crumbled, the reactor remains would still be unsafe for people to approach.

When the experimental Elk River reactor in Minnesota was closed down in 1968, it was dismantled. The cutting up of the heavy metal had to be done by remote control using a torch that could cut through steel under water. After the reactor was reduced to pieces small enough to bury, the cranes and cutting equipment were also buried. This problem of waste must make any society very wary of storing up such problems for future generations.

In Britain, the fact that is is quite legal for the nuclear power industry to lie has meant that the public has been deceived, as shown in my correspondence with the Advertising Standards Authority (page 40). Yet, despite this manipulation of the facts, when the Government wanted to privatise the electricity industry it had to cut nuclear power out of the arrangements.

So I would suggest that we develop three approaches to energy. The first point is that the poorest groups are often not able to afford enough heat for their needs. In cold winters, in both Britain and the

United States, there are elderly and disadvantaged people who die of hypothermia. We clearly need to alter the economic structure of society to ensure that such deprivation does not occur. So there are areas where there is a need for increased consumption.

However, on average, there is a need to reduce wasted consumption and to promote a lifestyle which uses less energy. One process which will reduce energy consumption is recycling. Britain is well behind other countries on this issue, although Leeds and Richmond have taken a lead and have recycling programmes. The latter has a slogan "Refuse what you can't re-use.' The heat generated during refuse incineration is used in many parts of the world. In Britain over 90% is buried, yet in Nottingham, a refuse incinerator provides heat for over 15,000 homes and other areas have begun to follow suit.

When I was a child we always used to separate our newspaper from the rest of the rubbish. This stopped when I was about the age of ten. Now, however, Friends of the Earth are starting new programmes for the collection of newspapers. In fact in April 1989, *The Independent* reported that the British government was about to promote a campaign to save waste paper. It said this costs only about £15 a tonne compared to £425 for new newsprint, so money would be saved and recycling would also reduce the mounting pressure on the landfills.

In Britain, recycling cans has been made more difficult because the cans are not labelled as to whether they are aluminium or steel. However, using the fact that aluminium is not magnetic, recycling is spreading. Recycling aluminium uses only ten per cent of the energy needed to process the virgin ore.

The second approach is a move towards public transport with the development of bus and train travel. The provision of bus lanes, will in many circumstances, lead to speedier travel. For those who drive there are a variety of means that can be employed to save energy. The first is to buy the car that is more energy efficient. There are good grounds not to buy a Rolls Royce because it does very few miles to the gallon. In an article on the prevention of global warming, the *New York Times* (3rd September 1989) discussed the possibility of energy saving cars which could achieve 138 miles per gallon. In the meantime, we can note that energy consumption is reduced by not accelerating too quickly and not driving too fast, trying whenever possible to walk or use public transport, and arranging to live nearby or on an easy route to places of work or college.

A third approach is to encourage the move towards renewable resources. Alcohol distilled from agricultural products is seen by many countries as the best alternative to imported oil. Brazil began its programme of producing alcohol from sugar cane in 1975 in order to reduce its dependence on imported oil. Currently, two thirds of its energy is supplied from renewable sources and it aims to become self-sufficient in fuel in 1990. There are potential problems with producing energy, rather than food crops. In Brazil, for example, there have been conflicts between the affluent city dwellers who want fuel for their cars and the rural poor.

Methane can also be obtained from sewage and agricultural waste, and can be used to power short range vehicles such as tractors and fork lift trucks. In Britain, some sewage works produce their own heat and light and there is great potential for farms to become self-sufficient in energy.

Another source of renewable energy is solar power. Enough energy from the sun reaches the top layers of the Earth's atmosphere in around thirty minutes to satisfy the needs of everyone for a year. About 30% of this energy is reflected — the rest is absorbed and provides the main source of heat in the lower atmosphere. Life is made possible by the soaking up of much of the ultraviolet and other short-wave radiation by the ozone layer. Without the ozone layer life on Earth would not be possible. Solar domestic hot water systems are technologically mature, economically feasible and usually designed to meet 80% of the demand of the household. Solar heating panels have also been developed extensively in the United States for swimming pools.

Solar power, together with the Earth's spin and the gravitational effect of the moon, creates the ocean movement and the energy that causes the great trade winds. So indirectly, windmills are a source of solar power. In Europe, windmills are closely identified with the Dutch who developed them in the tenth century after they originated in Iran in the seventh century. In a sense, the Netherlands were built by windmills which were used to pump water from land below sea level. In the United States, windmills were used to provide water for beef cattle production and also for the steam locomotives on the transcontinental routes. Wind power lost out in Europe to the steam engine, and in the United States to gasoline. However, interest is now reviving. California aims to get 10% of its energy from large wind farms by the end of the century and Friends of the Earth say that Britain has an ideal climate for wind power which could generate at least 20% of its electricity.

The power available from the wind varies. If the wind speed doubles, the power increases eightfold. One advantage of wind power is that it tends to complement solar power — when the wind is blowing there is usually no sun. In some places it might be possible to have the sun in the day and wind at night. Wind can also be combined with water, and when the wind blows it can be used to raise water to high reservoirs to be used as backup when the wind falls off.

Ways of using the tides as a source of energy have intrigued many inventors and in 1966, the first tidal electric plant came into operation on the La Rance estuary on the Brittany coast of France.

Power from wood is another source of secondary solar power which could grow in importance. Some fast-growing trees like sycamore and poplar can also sprout again from stumps. The United States has more energy stored in wood than it has in oil. This wood is also reducing the amount of carbon dioxide in the atmosphere, so it is important that stocks do not become depleted.

The Earth has a molten core and power from its radioactive decay has a long history as a source of energy. People in ancient times prized caves with warm springs and together with geysers and steam jets, they have been used for recreation, healing, cooking and heating. The development of steam turbines for electric power generation led to the first natural electric generation plant being built in Italy in 1904. The geysers near San Francisco are used to provide about a third of the city's needs. However, generally this source of energy has remained underdeveloped despite the fact that there is an enormous amount of energy stored in the Earth's crust.

In the future, humankind will have to increasingly rely on renewable energy. However, governments have treated such sources as the poor relation. For example in 1983/4, £11.3 million was spent on all the renewable energy sources together, while £206 million was given to the development of nuclear power.

This chapter has sought to show that in three important areas, optimum use is more important. These are food, transport and energy. On the subject of health, we shall again only need the optimum level of medical treatment. So in the major areas of life we do not need to satisfy ever-expanding wants, but make improvements within a generally stable situation.

AREAS WHERE SOCIAL LIFE COULD BE IMPROVED BY A REDUCTION IN CONSUMPTION

WEAPONS

a) Governmental

Governmental expenditure on armaments is highly irrational. The most common reason given to justify high expenditure is that it is for 'defence' and in recent years in Western Europe this has meant protection against the Soviet Union. However, the real level depends on the balance of political forces in a country and very little else. Finland, on the borders of the Soviet Union, in 1986 spent less than a third of the proportion of its wealth on the armed forces as did Britain and less than a quarter of that spent by the United States. In 1987 France spent more than twice as much on armaments as Italy, and it was four times the proportion of its government expenditure.

In 1987 Austria, Romania, Italy, Ireland and Malta all spent less than five per cent of government expenditure on armaments. In contrast Britain, Spain, Albania, Yugoslavia and Switzerland spent between 10% and 20% and West Germany, Greece and the United States spent over 20%. The United States expenditure was, in fact, 28.7%, well above the level of any other NATO country. In absolute terms, the United States' expenditure was eight times that of the second highest country West Germany, and nine times that of the United Kingdom which was third. The Soviet Union, which could not defeat its opponents in Afghanistan, is hardly likely to try and march into the United States. So a very strong case for the reduction in the sizes of armed forces can be made for many countries — especially the United States, where the presence of its troops in many different countries and waterways has led to accidents and reprisals.

b) Personal

In the United States it is widely believed that the constitution says something along the lines 'The right of the people to keep and bear arms shall not be infringed'. In fact, the US second amendment is as follows ''A well regulated militia being necessary to the security of a free state (in the generic sense), the right of the people to keep and bear arms shall not be infringed.' The formulators of the constitution were concerned that Congress might be inclined to dismantle the state militias at some future time. The section on the right to keep and bear arms therefore applied to the question of maintaining a militia. So Congress may create laws that regulate, heavily tax or even prohibit the personal ownership or use of weapons without constitutional obstruction. The strict control of personal weapons in societies is a development which will greatly reduce the number of accidents and spontaneous murders.

ALCOHOL

Although a report in *The Lancet* in the early Seventies suggested that a little alcohol may protect against heart attacks, there are signs that the level of consumption is now too high. The World Health Organisation stated in a report published in 1988 that there has been a great increase in alcohol consumption and related problems in recent decades and that is it important to emphasise just how extensive is the range of health problems caused. Not only the alcohol-dependence syndrome itself, but also many disabling, and sometimes fatal, physical and psychological conditions can be attributed either wholly or in part to excessive drinking. In addition, alcohol-related traffic accidents account for a significant proportion of deaths in many countries, especially amongst young people. Accidents at work, in the home and during sporting events are all more frequently related to alcohol consumption than is widely realised. In more general terms, excessive drinking disrupts family life and can also result in violence and neglect. Another area of concern is drinking by pregnant women which can damage the foetus. It is therefore clear that it is not only the heavy drinkers who are vulnerable.

In Britain, people consumed about twice as much alcohol in 1989 as they did twenty years earlier. Currently, the British medical profession is recommending that women drink no more than 14 units of alcohol a week — equivalent to fourteen glasses of wine or about seven pints of beer. Alcohol is less concentrated in men's bodies and their recommended limit is 21 units a week or twelve pints of beer. One in four men and one in twelve women exceed the 'safe' levels recommended by the medical colleges. In Britain, it was estimated in 1989 that 20% of men and 2% of women had a drink problem, but that women's drinking had been increasing at a faster rate. Convictions for drinking and driving amongst women increased by 225% between 1975 and 1985 compared to an increase of 45% for men. In 1979, cirrhosis of the liver was five times more common in men than in women, but by 1989 it was only twice as common.

Despite the acknowledged problems with alcohol, it is, in many respects, an aid to sociability. In Britain, going out for a drink is the single most popular social pastime and it has an important role for some people at times of stress. However, excessive consumption, especially over the longer periods, can cause adverse effects.

CIGARETTE SMOKING

Smoking makes your legs fall off. Nearly ten times as many people lose their legs because of smoking than through accidents. This is because smoking leads to arterial disease which restricts the blood flow and leads in a percentage of cases to gangrene and the necessity of amputation.

In Britain, smoking has begun to rise again. Between 1980 and 1984 it fell by 20% and then dropped more slowly until in 1988 it increased again by 2%. In 1989, the British Medical Association asked the Chancellor to put 24 pence on the price of each pack. This would represent a 16% increase. It argued that on average, 270 people are killed prematurely by cigarettes every day which is a total of 100,000 avoidable deaths each year mainly from cancer and heart disease. Britain has the highest death rate from lung cancer in the world, and nine out of ten cases are caused through smoking as are at least 20%

of the deaths from heart disease. The British Medical Association also stated that if no action was taken there would be an extra 2,000 deaths a year by 2025. However, the Chancellor decided not to raise the price at all, so the real cost was set to fall in line with the eight per cent inflation making a further increase in consumption likely.

Currently, just over a third of adults in the United Kingdom smoke, but the figures are two out of five for the 20-24 age group. The highest professional groups have a much smaller percentage of smokers than the lowest groups. Less than one in five professional men smoke compared to over two in five (43%) unskilled men. The class gradient is slightly less marked for women. Amongst the youngest age groups 15-16 years old, 27% of girls and 18% of boys smoke.

The research seemed to indicate that only the smokers themselves were affected. However, in 1981, a study was published by Dr Hirayama in Tokyo, which showed that the non-smoking wives of men who smoked twenty or more cigarettes a day were twice as likely to die from lung cancer than those who husbands did not smoke. This data and other research into 'passive' smoking has shown that people harm not only themselves, but that pregnant woman can damage the foetus and parents can damage their children. Also people in offices can suffer if their colleagues smoke. In more than four out of five of the states in the USA smoking is banned in hospitals, large stores, cinemas, government buildings, museums and on public transport.

In an article in *The Observer*, Jeremy Lawrence pointed out a number of myths about smoking in Britain.

- Most smokers think they run a greater risk of dying in a car accident. In fact they are twenty-five times as likely to die from a smoking-related disease.

- Most smokers think that only heavy smokers are at risk however a third of those who die have smoked fewer than twenty a day.

- While nearly all smokers know there is some link between smoking and lung cancer, half do not know that smoking causes *most* cases of lung cancer.

- Most smokers think that taking vitamins and minerals are more important to their health than giving up smoking.

- Nearly half of smokers believe that the habit 'cannot really be dangerous or the Government wouldn't allow it to be advertised'.

- Many smokers feel that it is not worth giving up because the damage has been done already. They do not realise that the risk of lung cancer rises with the length of time a person smokes but declines when they stop and is near normal after ten years.

So there is a need for more education and information. However, I have great sympathy for those trying to give up as tobacco is one of the most addictive drugs. Three out of four smokers want to stop, or have tried to stop, but it is not easy and only one in four men and one in three women succeed in giving up before they are sixty.

Returnable containers Increased use of returnable bottles and cans will lead to better quality containers being manufactured and to less rubbish. When Suffolk County in New York State was about to introduce a law insisting that a returnable deposit should be introduced for cans and bottles in 1981, a park ranger put his case for the new law. He said he found that bottles and cans made up anywhere from 50 to 65% of his garbage by bulk. This meant more time and energy expended by public employees to clean up litter which then went into rapidly filling landfills. He said that the over-burdened taxpayer paid the price.

So the recycling of bottles and cans is conserving precious resources, saving energy and trimming the time required to clean up despoiled parks, benches and roadways.

Other areas of reduction are discussed later in the book. The chapter on health will call for a reduction of unnecessary surgery, the chapter on crime will indicate that changes could be made to reduce theft with the consequent reduction in the need for preventative measures such as burglar alarms and safes.

CONCLUSION

This chapter has argued that we should move away from the idea that wealth needs to be ever-increasing. We should not spend all our time constantly consuming. More importantly, we should consider how people use their time and how to create a more caring world. The possession of goods should be returned to their rightful position — a subordinate role to enhance people's lives but not the 'be all and end all'.

Chapter 4

HEALTH OR WEALTH IN RICH COUNTRIES?

On the world level there are many countries which have an appallingly high number of premature deaths. In Malawi, the calculated average length of life for men is 38 and for women 41, which is about half the longevity of Iceland, Sweden and Japan. Other countries show similar problems. In 1987 the average length of life for people in Afghanistan, Ethiopia and Sierra Leone was only 42 years. In Guinea it was 43 and in Angola, Mali and Niger it was 45 (*New Internationalist* Oct. 1989). The problem of world poverty is to be discussed in Chapter Six. Here I want to concentrate on the problems of Britain and the United States; both these countries need to change their systems in order to put them in a position where they provide the best health care possible.

FOUR YEARS WASTED IN BRITAIN AND THE UNITED STATES

The life expectancy of men in Iceland increased from 66.1 in 1941-50 to 70.7 in 1966-70 and to 75.0 in 1986. Furthermore many people in Iceland die prematurely. In Britain and the USA, the comparable figure for length of life was only 71 years. This could be due to genetic factors. However, we know there are a great number of excess deaths due to poor social conditions, inadequate health care, poor eating habits, drug abuse and a poor lifestyle. It is likely that, taken together, the social conditions could be altered to improve the length of life by a minimum of four years.

GROWTH AND HEALTH

There are those who believe that by increasing the wealth of society, health will automatically improve as more money will be available for better quality equipment. However, this is by no means the case. There are three central problems with health systems. The first is that they are too closely linked to the profit motive. This can lead to a polluted environment and subsequently adverse effects on health. Secondly, the links with the profit motive often leads to a series of problems. The drug industry spends a great deal of money advertising its wares to the medical profession and this in turn leads to an over reliance on drugs. In addition the profit motive can mean a great deal of excess surgery for the rich and inadequate treatment for the poor. Thirdly, there is the problem of the medical nature of care. I will now further consider these three areas.

Health and the environment

In the earlier chapters I suggested a variety of improvements in the environment that would benefit the health of the community. The promotion of public transport would lead to less individual travel with its high accident rate. In Britain, for example, the death rate per billion passenger kilometres for the years 1976-86 was 0.3 for rail, 0.8 for bus or coach yet 5.9 for car. So cars are almost twenty times as dangerous as trains. Additional benefits include the exercise involved in walking to and from buses and trains and the improvement in the quality of the air that would result from a reduction in the number of cars. It can be seen that the health of the community would be improved by the promotion of public transport.

The pollution of air in towns leads to higher rates of lung cancer than in in the surrounding countryside and also affects other lung diseases. The poor quality of water in some areas also leads to ill health with chemicals leaking into the water supply. For example, high rates of aluminium can cause Alzheimer's disease. As we have seen, the quality of food is also wanting in many respects and advertising often encourages unhealthy eating patterns. The promotion of a healthy diet with alcohol taken in moderation and tobacco not at all, would help to achieve a healthier society.

Many occupations have an adverse affect on health. Lesley Doyal in *The Political Economy of Health* (1985 edition) discusses the high rate of industrial illness in Britain. One estimate is that two thousand die each year of injuries received at work. About 30,000 miners still suffer some kind of lung disease and they have about a one in five chance of being injured at work in any one year. Very often there are conflicts between safety and increased profits which lead to unnecessary risks being taken.

It is the manual workers who suffer the greatest likelihood of physical injury but the middle classes also suffer stress from what is often characterised as 'the rat race'. Heart disease is one of the biggest killers and for many people their work is such that it is likely to cause this kind of illness. One doctor wrote to *World Medicine* that the way to prevent heart disease is to look at work loads and lifestyles imposed by companies to see if something needs to be done in that area. This is an important point and there is no real reason why so many jobs have to be stressful.

A move towards a more caring society will reduce anxiety and promote a positive attitude to life. There is a great deal of evidence that the happier and more contented people are with their lives, the better their health is likely to be. One study in the US Navy showed that out of 2,500 men, those who had experienced problems such as divorce or money worries were much more likely to be ill than those who had not faced these problems. This fact ties in with what I said in earlier chapters about the benefits of working for a better and happier world where people are at unity with nature and themselves. If people have good relationships and realistic goals, they are likely to be happier and healthier. So the changes in society proposed in this book would have a positive effect on the overall health of the community.

Drug culture in medicine

The dominant medical practice is very drug-orientated and can be criticised on this account. The average British patient receives six prescriptions a year from the doctor and there is also a large market in over-the-counter drugs. Some drugs have caused widely publicised problems. In the early Sixties, thalidomide was given to pregnant women to reduce the effects of morning sickness. In many cases it damaged the foetus and led to the birth of many deformed children in Europe. It was banned in the United States and President Kennedy awarded a gold medal to the woman who prevented its use. Some people believe this was an isolated incident. However, there is a strong argument that this damage was only the tip of the iceberg.

The Natural Medicines Society argues that the deaths from medically prescribed drugs are higher than those from road accidents. It also draws attention to a World Health Organisation Report which says that only 26 drugs are of use and only nine are essential. Yet there are 25,000 in use worldwide.

There are numerous other drugs which have caused problems. In fact the authors of the book *Cured to Death: the effects of prescription drugs* argue that major drug tragedies continue to kill or maim thousands. Overall, an estimated one million cases of adverse drug reaction occur in Britain each year. There are far too many drugs in use for them all to have undergone rigorous testing. The birth-control pill is probably one of the best tested of the drugs available but still its long term effects are being discovered. Other drugs are not tested to such a degree and so their effects are largely unknown.

In an interview, a London based practitioner of alternative medicine pointed out that the drugs industry is the largest in the world. He also told me that even drugs which have been tested when put on the market have killed or maimed: *'Over fifty drugs have been withdrawn. For example the International Herald Tribune in 1978 reported the ban on the drug atromid S. which aimed to reduce cholesterol. The makers said they would protest the ban. One major finding was that long term users did not have lower rates of heart attacks but had increased deaths from cancer and other illnesses.'*

Another example he gave was that of oxychinol which was a drug sold under 168 different brand names and was supposed to treat diarrhoea. The company — Ciba Geigy — disregarded adverse tests on animals in which, for example, dogs developed epileptic fits. The drug led to 1000 deaths in Japan and 30,000 cases of blindness or paralysis of lower limbs. The Swedish doctor who exposed the drug commented 'Some big drug manufacturers do not hesitate to walk over human corpses for profits'.

I asked him how alternative medicine differed from the conventional kind and he told me he preferred the term 'Naturopathic medicine'. He said it differs in that it treats the whole person and aims to attack the cause rather than the symptons. *A doctor seeing a person with a sore throat will deal only with that but the naturopathic practitioner will find out what is causing the problem.* He continued to say that the techniques have been used for thousands of years and commented that ancients knew the effects by empirical evidence and recognised the curative properties of plants.

The medical profession has been largely opposed to any infringement of its territory by those who specialise in treatment without the use of drugs. An editorial in the *British Medical Journal* in December 1985 attacked alternative practitioners for using ineffective and destructive techniques on a gullible public. It was criticised in March 1986 when a correspondent pointed out that freely selected homeopathic remedies were scientifically shown to be effective in the treatment of rheumatoid arthritis. A BMA report published in 1986 also recognised that some people benefit from acupuncture and said in more general terms that some of the multitude of techniques may be therapeutic and also that osteopathy may relieve pain, However, it argued that homeopathy appeared to be successful as a cure partly due to the beliefs of the practitioner being communicated to the patient and partly to the appearance of the medicine. This overall dismissive attitude suggests that a more open minded approach to all kinds of help is likely, in the long term, to broaden horizons and improve health.

This third problem is the idea that treatment is something that only doctors and nurses give to patients. This, combined with the pressures of the market and the drug companies, has led to a great deal of unnecessary intervention. This can be seen from childbirth, which is clearly the most fundamental of all experiences. Yet this natural process has increasingly become a medical event. Women are usually made to give birth lying on their backs despite the serious disadvantages of this position. In the United States women were routinely cut before birth, despite the fact that, when scientifically tested, episiotomy was found to be unnecessary. They are also commonly given drugs to ensure their child is born during social hours, regardless of the fact that induced births are more painful. Caesarean births are often performed for the same reason. In addition, the pressure for profits from inventions and drugs means that hospitals and doctors are influenced to use the most advanced technical equipment at great cost and very often without proper analysis of the benefits. Foetal monitors are a good example. They were successfully marketed but introduced with few doctors knowing how to use them which led to many unnecessary Caesareans. So here again, the pursuit of profits can conflict with good health care.

WHERE DOCTORS CAUSE PROBLEMS

In its report considering alternative medicine, the *British Medical Journal* claimed that orthodox medicine *'has led to large, demonstrable, and reproducible benefits for mankind, on a scale which alternative therapies cannot match'* (Vol 296 p1407).

However, there are critics of this rosy view even from within the ranks of the medical profession. Rene Dubo, an eminent bacteriologist who held a chair in the Rockefeller University, New York, discovered an antibiotic. In his book *Mirage of Health* (1959) he points out that the achievements of medicine are not all that some would like to claim. He argues that the main credit for the eradication of destructive epidemics should go to the social reformers who work for better sewage and improved living conditions.

Ivan Illich, author of *Limits to Medicine* , goes further and claims the medical profession is a threat to health. He also argues that the health services have not been the main factor in the improvements in the length of life in recent years. As an example he says that the New York death rate from tuberculosis in 1812 was estimated at above 700 per 10,000 but by 1882, when Koch first isolated and cultured the bacillus, it had already declined to 370 and to 180 when the first sanatorium was opened. Furthermore, 90% of the reduction in deaths from childhood illnesses such as whooping cough, measles, scarlet fever and diptheria between 1860 and 1965 occurred before the introduction of immunisation and antibiotics. He states the major factor was improved nutrition followed by improved housing and a decrease in the virulence of the micro organisms.

He recognises that medicine has developed some successful cures. Antibiotics reduced pneumonia, gonorrhea and syphilis. Immunisation has wiped out paralytic poliomyelitis. These facts and others help to confirm the popular belief in 'medical progress'. But other things have not changed. He claims mortality for 90% of cancers has remained unchanged for the past twenty-five years. The exceptions are skin cancer and cervical cancer. He says the five year survival of breast cancer is 50% regardless of the frequency of medical check ups. Illich is right to draw our attention to the fact that there can be great improvements in health by changing the social conditions, indeed this is one of my central contentions. He is also correct to point out that successes in medicine frequently get trumpeted while the failures in treatment often receive scant publicity in the media. However, Illich is overstating the case. There have also been improvements in the treatment of leukaemia and in Hodgkins disease which he neglects to mention.

Illich's argument goes further than this, however. He says the use of futile medical treatment is one fact but the pain dysfunction, disability and anguish resulting from technical medical intervention causes many deaths. In addition, he states that every day about half the US population swallow a medically prescribed pill which often causes them harm. The average American adult also swallows over two hundred aspirins a year. Furthermore, Illich states that one in five patients in teaching hospitals receive a medically induced disease.

We do not have to agree with Illich on the extent of the damage done by the medical profession. He does tend to ignore the benefits that can come from such operations as hip replacements or the techniques the profession has developed for resetting limbs. However, there clearly are medical scandals and one of these is unnecessary surgical intervention. One example, on which I have carried out research since 1978, is the Caesarean rate.

UNNECESSARY DEATHS FROM CAESAREANS

A problem particularly facing the United States is the damage from unnecessary operative deliveries. There are at least 142 deaths from unnecessary Caesareans each year in the United States according to the Public Citizen Health Research Group. This organisation, which is linked to the Ralph Nader organisation, bases its claim on the fact that Caesareans in the United States are four times as dangerous as normal childbirth where only one in ten thousand women die giving birth. Overall in 1986, 24% of US births were by Caesarean section which is up from 5.5% in 1970. They estimated the rate was twice as high as necessary and the spokesman, Dr Sidney Wolfe, called it *the number one unnecessary surgery in the United States*. In fact, I would suggest that even a Caesarean rate of 10% is higher than is justified by the present level of medical knowledge which is an indication of just how bad the situation is.

Dr Wolfe stated that women had not been adequately informed of all the extra risks and costs and argued that if this information was made widely available to the public then the rate would come down. I feel, however, that he was unduly optimistic. I became interested in the issue when my daughter was about to be born on Long Island, New York. We attended the special courses for expectant parents to prepare them for the birth and to socialise them into believing that the hospital's way of doing things is best. The woman leading the session, told our group that one in three of the women were going to need a Caesarean. She was actually wrong — it was one in four — but as I knew the latest British figures were only about 5%, I was shocked and I decided to carry out research into the subject. The British rates have also increased, but only from 3.1% in 1963 to about 11% in 1986. So the US mothers have to suffer more than twice the risk of a Caesarean than their British counterparts.

One of the arguments often used to justify a high Caesarean rate is that it leads to a reduction in child deaths around the time of birth. However, Dr O'Driscol published an article in the *Journal of the American College of Obstetrics and Gyneacology* which showed that over a fifteen year period, the infant deaths in Dublin had dropped from 42 per thousand to 17 per thousand while the Caesarean rate remained constant at between four and five per cent. The Irish infant death rates were then below comparable United States levels. Evidence from other countries supports this. Holland, for example, in the early Eighties had only a fifth of the US Caesarean rate but had many fewer infant deaths. The reasons for the growth in Caesareans are linked to other factors.

From the evidence of the previous births, we can deduce one factor, — it is very convenient for the doctor. Pre-planned Caesareans in particular are quicker for the doctor and are more lucrative. They also occur during social hours.

An important point likely to affect Caesarean rates is the relative status of the woman giving birth and the practitioner. If the status of the person attending the birth is much higher than that of the expectant mother, then the time of the attender will be considered very valuable. This can act to prevent the best care being given. This is one factor behind the high American Caesarean rate. Two American doctors have explained to women why they should not expect a vaginal birth after a Caesarean and their reasoning had nothing to do with good medical care:'*Instead of spending the time in the office seeing other patients while you are labouring, the physician must spend many hours exclusively with you at a time that may be totally inconvenient. Your delivery may take as long as ten hours out of the doctor's day or night, while a repeat Caesarean would take only an hour or so* '.

So we can see from this candid quotation how status interacts with financial factors. In countries like Holland where midwives carry out a large number of the deliveries, the Caesarean rates are much lower. The quote also shows how financial factors act to the detriment of good care. The doctor not only performs a Caesarean in a shorter time than a normal delivery, but also is paid more. The doctor is also less likely to be sued following a Caesarean. So it is something of a surprise that the United States rate is not even higher. Doctors attending rich women in Brazil have certainly seen the financial benefits from Caesareans and more than 80% of deliveries to the better off insured groups are by this method.

A second reason for the rise in Caesareans is the threat of litigation. Dr Pennington, a New York obstetrician, said that if there are any problems with the birth then the doctor can be sued. However, if an unnecessary Caesarean was to be carried out and the woman died, it would be considered a normal risk of the operation. Despite the fact that the British Caesarean rates are below half those in New York, there are nevertheless many that are unnecessary and carried out through fear of litigation. In a survey in the late 1980's this was one of the major comments made by obstetricians. John McGarry, a highly-regarded British consultant was not due to take part in the survey but he saw the questionnaire and wrote:

> 'Incidentally I saw your name on a Maternity Alliance question form that one of my colleagues has completed. He says that the Caesarean section rate has gone up because we are operating on smaller and smaller babies and that this has caused the salvage rate to go up. I am afraid that the gentleman is utterly deluded. Our Caesarean rate has gone up 300% in the fifteen years I have been here and yet the salvage of small babies has not changed one jot. The reason that the Caesarean section rate is going up is that we are all scared stiff of litigation '.

Many other doctors made similar points in the survey and the situation is, of course, much worse in the United States. One of the points I made in an interview with the *Sunday Times* (9 October 1988) was that when doctors do Caesareans because of fear of litigation, the women involved are not informed. They are given reasons such as foetal distress or the cord was round the baby's neck etc. to avoid them discovering the truth. This deception is highly unsatisfactory. There is a way to solve the problem — this is to introduce no-fault compensation for birth injuries. If parents have to bring up a child with problems, they need help whether or not the doctor was to blame.

Another reason for the increase in Caesareans is that it has become a medical fashion. There is evidence that a number of doctors in England see Caesareans as the birthing method of the future. The rise in the number in Britain was preceded in 1975 by a quote from two obstetricians, Sutherst and Case, in a major English medical journal where they said that induction and acceleration of labour are not just progress in medical terms but are socially acceptable to both mother and obstetrician. They continued to say that it was more satisfactory to the mother if she knows exactly when she is going to have her baby so that she can, for example, arrange for her husband to have holiday time off work or to get relatives to look after other children. They suggested that not only was the induction of labour likely to become more available, but Caesareans might well be contemplated for the same reasons. The change might be such that, during the next forty years, the allowing of a vaginal delivery might have to be justified and become the exception rather than the rule. In the United States in the late Seventies, there were often battles in hospitals between the obstetricians who wished to follow the desires of the vast majority of women for as little intervention as possible, and those who wanted to intervene on every possible occasion. The time has come for a concerted effort to reduce the Caesarean rates down to the optimum level in the best interests of both mothers and babies.

THE POOR DIE YOUNG

The largest gaps in health are between the rich and poor countries, but even within developed countries there are wide differences between classes in mortality rates. There would be a great improvement in overall health if these could be reduced. The class differences are, in all probability, much greater in the United States than other countries. A report in *Newsday* (29 Aug 1989) stated that nationwide in 1986, black infants were twice as likely to die as white infants. However, the latest local data for Suffolk County for 1988 showed that 17.9 of every 1,000 black babies died in the first year of life compared to only 7.1 white babies. In Nassau County, the black death rate was much higher at 31.2 per thousand — more than four times the white rate.

A report in the *New England Journal of Medicine* (24 Aug 1989) commented that poor children in the United States faced a higher rate of mortality and morbidity than more affluent children. They also faced more tuberculosis, mental illness, nutritional deficiency, spina bifida, lead poisoning and anaemia. It continued to say: *'To be born poor in this wealthy nation is to face more than one's fair share of risk and illness'.*

In Britain too, despite the ideology of equal treatment, there are many social differences in health. A major government sponsored report *The Black Report* was published in August 1980. This documented the inequalities in health between the social classes. It found that for working men aged between 15-65, those in the two highest classes — professional and managerial — had almost half the mortality ratio of those in the lowest social groups of semi-skilled and unskilled workers. For women, the differences according to class is narrower than for men.

The infant mortality rates showed even greater class gradients, with children of unskilled workers being more than two and a half times as likely to die in the first year of life as the children of professional workers. Commenting on the report, the government minister, Patrick Jenkin, spoke of the failure to reduce class inequalities and the fact that they might be increasing. He said the group found that the causes of health inequalities were so deep-rooted that only a major and wide-ranging programme of public expenditure would be capable of altering the pattern.

He also said that additional expenditure on the scale corresponding to the report's recommendations — the amount involved could be upwards of £2 billion a year — would be quite unrealistic in the present or any forseeable future economic circumstances and that he could not therefore endorse the Group's recommendations.

The *British Medical Journal* criticised the Government's attitude:

> ' It may be true that the Government cannot at present provide the money for an ideal policy. . .That is no reason, however, for the Secretary of State failing to look at the pattern of services which could be developed even within present resource limitations.' (20 Sept 1980)

As the Government decided that it was not going to take action against these class differences an opportunity was lost to take action to improve the overall health of the community.

THE AMERICAN HEALTH SCANDAL

'Without health we are nothing' said the *Los Angeles Times* in an article on the 21 August 1988 but it went on to say that the country was in a health care crisis it had never before experienced. Earlier in the month, it had reported the fact that Blue Cross had increased its premiums by 25% and at the same time reduced benefits. The article continued to document the fact that a major Los Angeles hospital had decided not to accept ambulances on the grounds that it was too costly and that the hospitals in California had lost two billion dollars in the last year from poor payment of bills. Overall, half the hospitals were losing money and six more were threatening not to take emergencies. Sam Tibbet, the head of a company that runs fourteen hospitals, commented that soon the national debt and trade imbalance would pale by comparison. The time had come for the Government to compensate for the situation it had created and set up a state and national policy. The New York Times said in October 1988 that 40% of the nation's 5,728 hospitals lose money when treating patients on medicare. It pointed to the fact that Washington DC General could not operate 46 of its beds because of shortage of funds.

Reports in other areas have exposed similar worries. An article in the Chicago Tribune in January 1988 documented various problems. It noted that millions had no health insurance and said these 'constitute a population of medical outcasts' who get little or nothing from the wonders or even the basics of modern medicine. It noted the ineffectiveness of the market place and called for national health insurance which, it said, would have problems but would be preferable to the current situation where vast expenditures are not producing commensurate results while large parts of the population are cruelly denied basic care. These two reports were echoed by a third in the New York Times which pointed out that in Texas, only those who earn 34% less than the national poverty level can get medical aid, and that many travelled to Mexico for their treatment for financial reasons. There, the care might not be as good, but at least people could afford it. The very poorest get medicaid, but this does not cover expensive operations such as transplants. In Virginia in 1988 a liver transplant cost £110,000, so poor people who needed one simply died.

The number without health care has risen from 29 million in 1980 to 37 million in 1988. One third of those without health insurance are children. These are not the very impoverished who will be covered by medicaid for some care, but those with struggling parents caught in the early years of parenthood going down from two incomes to one, having to face the cost of childbirth, the high mortgages of the early years of married life and the problems of rearing children in a society which is comparatively unsupportive. The elderly can get medicare which covers some of their costs but by no means all.

WHY THE MARKET DOES NOT WORK IN HEALTH

A major problem with the American system is that it relies too much on market forces and, while previous chapters have shown these do not work well in large parts of the economy, in the area of health they have particular difficulties. *The Chicago Times* rightly said *'medical care, unlike a vacation package, is an anxiety filled need that does not evoke bargain hunting tactics amongst most people'*. This is true. If you buy cheap apples at a market you can decide to buy some more. If they are not of sufficient quality you can buy elsewhere next time. However, with crucial health decisions you cannot possibly have the information as to the qualifications of the best doctor. The only way to have the best treatment for one is to have the best treatment for all.

One problem with insurance is that companies really prefer the healthy to those who are ill. They want to eliminate bad risks. This leads to two problems. First, the sick are likely to get inferior treatment because they may be too ill to work and therefore too poor to afford the proper care. Secondly the rich may be milked for whatever funds they have available. Bunker showed in an article in the *New England Journal of Medicine* in 1970 that people in the United States had twice as many operations per head as those in Britain. This was largely due to the fact that people in the States were having unnecessary surgery. The fact that doctors were being paid, not for the quality of their work as are consultants in Britain, but on the number of operations they carry out, meant that they were able to maximise their income by carrying out more surgery. Consequently such operations as tonsillectomies and hysterectomies were far more common than they should have been. Women in the United States are four times more likely to have a hysterectomy than women in Britain. One problem with private insurance is that once people have paid the premium, they have an incentive to consume as much as can be obtained under the policy. The doctor, too, stands to benefit the most by recommending the most expensive treatment possible. So in many cases, the patient and doctor are in a position where they both want to make the treatment expensive.

Bunker's article appeared before the large rise in Caesareans and so the situation seems to have deteriorated further. The American people have to suffer far too much surgery than is compatible with good health and their system of healthcare needs to be changed radically.

Not surprisingly, the health costs in the US have continued to rise out of all proportion to other areas. It increased from 5.3% of Gross National Product in 1960 to 11.4% in 1987. The absolute rise in costs was much greater even allowing for inflation. The increase has been such that the elderly now pay a greater proportion of their income on health care than they did in the days before medicare became available. One of the reasons for this, according to the *Daily Mail* , is that hospitals have undergone the medical equivalent of the arms race with hospitals vying with each other for the most expensive equipment. Because of this ten hospitals in St Louis offer open heart surgery.

Another reason for spiralling health costs may well be crime. *Newsday* (4 September 1989) gave a number of examples from New York State.

★ A doctor purchased blood from poor people and junkies and then billed medicaid $3.6 million for unnecessary and expensive blood tests.

★ Two shoe store owners sold cheap sneakers and work boots but charged medicaid for $520,000 worth of expensive orthopedic shoes.

★ A psychiatrist billed medicaid for 3,000 phantom visits by real patients and collected $75,000 in illegal fees.

★ A clinic owner and his sons frauded medicaid of $16 million over seven years with hundreds of thousands of phony billings.

These examples are probably only the tip of the iceberg and indicate the problems that can occur when financial interests are paramount.

One of the ideas behind a free market in health is that it will lead to greater choice. The evidence simply does not support this. The crucial difference between a doctor and, say, an insurance salesman is that when you see the salesman you are the one making the decision about whether you need the benefit. With medicine, under a fee for service system, the doctor both makes the diagnosis and stands to benefit if the decision is for intervention. How much better to have a doctor whose income is secured and whose only interest lies in the best treatment for you. Another problem, leading to financial restraints reducing choice, is that most insurance companies now insist that the patient contact them before going into hospital, and may, in some circumstances, decide which doctor the patient can use and which hospital can be attended. The British system has much greater freedom than this.

Another factor is that if the general level of care is low, then there may be nowhere to go. In 1980 I carried out research into unnecessary Caesareans in Massachussets, and I found that in all the state's hospitals the rate was higher than the average for Britain. So, in contrast to Britain, there was no choice for a woman which would offer a low risk of medical intervention. Also in many parts of the United States there are virtually no doctors who will make a home visit. Here again choice is lower than in Britain.

One of the big changes in the United States in recent years is the large increase in day care or outpatient treatment which the insurers hoped would reduce costs. According to the *New York Times* , this 87 increased from 19% of the treatment in 1981 to 40% in 1986 and is a key factor in the US hospital bed occupancy being only 67% in 1987. Here again, the influence of cost cutting means that the individual's choices are frustrated.

The advantage of not having to be concerned with financial matters is that doctors can spend their working time concentrating on providing the best health care possible and allows them time to keep up with the latest information and advances in order to renew their skills.

From the consumer angle, the question of health insurance is a thorny problem. On the 23 October 1988 the *New York Times* quoted an expert as saying that people feel threatened both by financial medical catastrophe and by a bewildering array of complex insurance products. The *Chicago Times* said in January 1988 that 'It's getting harder to be a savvy patient and to make sure of good medical care as the rules and ways of paying hospitals keep changing'. As an example of one of the problems that can occur, the *Los Angeles Times* in August told of how a woman, insured with Blue Cross, decided she would increase her 'deductable', (the amount she would pay before the insurance company would take over) from $1,000 to $2,000 to save herself money. When she had completed the change, however, Blue Cross then considered her a new customer. She then had to pay more money than if she had not tried to reduce her outlay.

For those who do not have health insurance or have insufficient cover, there can be terrible problems. At the time the person is ill and cannot work, there is the added stress of high hospital bills, guilt about the added expense to the family budget and sometimes financial disaster. Forty per cent of the personal bankruptcies in the United States are attributable to debts for medical care. For those who experience long term illness in their old age, they see their money gradually run out as they are faced with high medical and nursing home bills. The knowledge that this can happen brings a great deal of insecurity to American society, even amongst the healthy. Except for the mega rich, there is no means of absorbing the costs of a long term serious illness which will lead to great financial problems.

The major insurance companies tried to stop the level of unnecessary surgery by introducing second opinions. However, the second opinion was often just as interventionist as the first and therefore did not justify the extra cost.

To help keep down costs and the tendency for excess surgery, Health Maintenance Organisations have been developed. They are run by an insurance company or a collection of doctors who agree to provide complete health care for groups of people at roughly 30% below normal prices. The HMO's sign up a panel of doctors who are willing to work for less than their usual fee to get a bulk supply of patients. The patients forfeit the right to see a doctor of their choice and the place of treatment. Forty per cent of HMO's are losing money and some of them have tried to cut costs by increasing the payment to the doctor for reduced treatment levels. The doctor then becomes the gatekeeper of care.

In January 1988, the *New England Journal of Medicine* considered this development. It said that physicians have been shown to respond to various financial incentives and talked of the problem of the conflict between the doctor's financial interest and the welfare of the patients. In some ways the situation is just the opposite of what happens in fee for service, for with HMOs, doctors are being paid more to do less. The journal proposed that patients could get some protection against lack of treatment by requiring HMO's to inform members of financial inducements. However, my suggestion is that if the USA wants to improve its care, it should move away from such over emphasis on cost and towards a system where doctors are rewarded, not for giving more treatment, nor for giving less treatment, but for giving the best treatment.

One of the points that has arisen from research into comparative costs is that competition does not lead to lower prices. Daniel Greenberg, writing in the *Chicago Times* in January 1988, stated that the health industry has recognised this and responded to it by promoting more costly services. It reported that a study of neighbouring hospitals found, for example, that their bills ran higher than those of isolated hospitals because they offered more competitive services in order to attract doctors and patients. The article continued to state that, freed from legal restraint, the medical advertising focused increasingly on selling to new markets in fields ranging from obstreperous children to obesity control.

Some people believe that private enterprise is more efficient than state-run businesses but the evidence in respect of health care does not support this. For example, the Director of Britain's Institute of Health Service Management said in 1987 that the cost of managing the British Health Service was only 4.5% of the budget compared to 12% in France and 21% in the United States. The president of the corporation which owns the John Hopkins Hospital in Baltimore explained to a reporter from the *Daily Mail* that, when a person arrives at the hospital without medical insurance then 'the bureaucracy involved is overwhelming'. They try to find out whether they can pay 25% of the costs. If people fail to pay, the hospital's debt collectors pursue them energetically.

The United States can afford a health care system with benefits for all even if it were simply an integrated system of insurance such as that in Massachussets. In fact, it is the only developed country without one. The fear of taxes is one factor mentioned, as is faith in the market. In addition a major underlying reason seems to be that the country has an inordinate fear of government intervention. It seems to believe the propaganda from the extreme right-wing that public provision is necessarily inefficient and bureaucratic. This simply is not the case. The British health system is very efficient. The collection of money by taxes is by far the cheapest and easiest way and absolves doctors from a great deal of unnecessary form filling.

HOW THE LAWYERS STOP GOOD HEALTH CARE

The head of one of New York's maternity services told me that the medical profession had begun to 'hate' lawyers. He said 'I can barely bring myself to talk to one if we meet at a party'. He added that at first they just used to attack the medical profession for taking the wrong action but now, if that charge does not stick, they argue that the doctor had not taken the right action early enough.

The problems with malpractice in the United States are not new. Richard Titmuss pointed out that as long ago as 1969, one in five American physicians had been sued for malpractice. However, in recent years the problem has become much worse. In one group of 3,000 doctors in New York State, 30% had a claim notified against them in one year. In 1987 insurance premiums were over £50,000 for obstetricians and £10,000 for family doctors in contrast to £576 in Britain for General Practitioners. So the average doctor in the United States was paying about sixteen times more for malpractice insurance as a comparable English doctor. These costs would, of course, be passed on to the patients. Fear of lawyers also meant extra tests for the purpose of defensive medicine.

Although the problem of litigation is much less important in Britain, it is still a problem which needs to be dealt with by change in policy.

BRITISH HEALTH CARE

The main strength of the British system is primarily that it is universal. Everybody in the country qualifies for free treatment. It is also efficient. Expenditure on administration is lower as a proportion of the budget than that of other major countries. Its management costs are lower than virtually all the other major enterprises, either inside or outside the public sector.

The method of obtaining treatment is, in the first instance, to go to either the local General Practitioner (GP) or, in a case of emergency to the local hospital. Both these services are free and the majority of patients stay with the same general practitioner for many years and so build up a relationship. General practitioners are paid a capitation fee for each registered patient and so have very little financial advantage in giving extra treatment. They can, however, charge for a physical examination for an insurance policy and also receive a fee from the Government for birth control services. However, these services are free to women. The general practitioners are specialised in diagnosis and will see many cases during the course of a day. Most doctors have now arranged themselves in group practices and have a timetable worked out so that one doctor is on call while the others have their holidays or a weekend off. The doctors may carry out antenatal care and also deliveries, either at the woman's home or, more likely, at the local hospital where there is a GP unit. Most GP's have spent 3 years working at a hospital but have a different role from the average American doctor. The doctor in the United States will normally treat the patient in a local hospital. The patient will pay one fee to the doctor and another 'hotel type' fee to the hospital. The British doctor who finds something that cannot be dealt with at the surgery will then refer the patient to the hospital under the care of the relevant staff.

At the top of the British system of care are the highly paid consultants. These receive a salary and may also be give a merit award on top of this. A third of British consultants have this merit award and the most generous of these, A +, can double their NHS salary. The consultants (specialists) are appointed generally in their late thirties after a long period of hospital training and research under other consultants and after having gained further (Royal College Membership) qualifications. Full time consultants can earn up to 10% of their salary from private sector work. Each patient entering a hospital is placed under the care of a consultant who is in charge of a team called a firm. The second highest position within the firm is held by the senior registrar who is on a fixed term contract and who hopes, in time, to be appointed a consultant. Third in line are the registrars of which there may be several in one firm. The registrars and senior registrars carry out many of the operations and the consultant is responsible for monitoring all the work in the firm and ensuring it is of a sufficiently high standard. Each firm is relatively independent, having internal rules for the division of labour which are determined by the consultant.

Hospitals have regular meetings of consultants where problems such as avoidable deaths are discussed and suggestions made as to how care can be maintained and improved. I spoke to Harold Schulman, the Head of Obstetrics at Winthrop University Hospital on Long Island, who said that he was envious of the position held by British consultants because their time could be concentrated on the difficult problems they were the best able to sort out. However, this is not to deny that there are problems with the British system. Some are similar to those in the United States, however, others are different.

One characteristically British problem is the waiting time that exists for non urgent surgery. The main reason for this is under-financing rather than an intrinsic fault in the structure of the system. In the early 1980's, many hospitals were placed under cash limits, some were closed and others had to restrict the amount of surgery they could perform. In fact, the standard textbook on NHS funding published by the *Accountants Educational Trust* in 1987 argued that the Government under-financed the health service in order to engineer a cutback in service. The abolition of free eye tests and dental checks was imposed to save minimal amounts of money and yet hit hardest those just above the poverty line.

A key area for analysis which could affect many people is kidney disease. One estimate was that 2,000 people die unecessarily each year in Britain because of lack of care (*The Guardian* 17 October 1987). There have been a few attempts to protest this situation and Professor Stewart Cameron at Guy's supported a campaign to encourage hospital doctors to refuse to sign death certificates for patients who died as a direct result of health cuts. However, there has not been a concerted and well organised campaign of the kind that the women's groups mounted over natural childbirth.

I met several people in the United States who had heard that people in Britain could not get treatment for kidney disease if they were over the age of sixty. They usually saw this as one of the failures of what they call 'socialised medicine.'

Shortages have other effects. Wendy Savage, consultant obstetrician at the London Hospital, has told me of a number of recent cases in her experience where women have been transferred while in labour. For example, when she was duty consultant, a woman 27 weeks pregnant was transferred from one hospital, due to the lack of cots, to the London Hospital five miles away where she gave birth prematurely to twins. The next problem was that the London Hospital had only one cot available, so one of the babies had to be transferred to another hospital. The mother had to take a taxi each time she wanted to visit her. In another example, a woman was transferred by ambulance in premature labour from the London to a north London Hospital where there were cots available. When her labour ceased, the hospital sent her back to the London on the Tube.

In 1975 the Government set the target that all urgent cases should be admitted to hospital within one month and all non urgent cases within a year. However, the present government has hopelessly failed on this. The latest detailed data available for September 1986 showed that 61% of urgent cases had been on the waiting list for more than a month and 26% of non urgent cases had been waiting more than a year. The situation has deteriorated if anything since then and the officially published opinion polls show that the percentage of people dissatisfied with the National Health Service increased from a quarter (25%) in 1983 to nearly two in five (30%) in 1987.

The Accountants Educational Trust became concerned that the Government planned to encourage private medicine by using long waiting lists as the big stick to encourage people to join insurance plans. An advert from the Automobile Association states simply and directly *'What would YOU do if you needed hospital treatment, but there were around 800,000 on the NHS waiting list already '*. I saw this kind of advertisement as aiding government strategy, and began a campaign against such adverts. The following article appeared in my local newspaper in February 1989 and I sent a copy to various Members of Parliament with whom I had had previous contact.

'A lecturer had retaliated to a mailshot offering private medical insurance by donating £15 a month to local hospital. Colin Francome, 44, was so appalled by the AA's Hospital Plan brochure he has made out a direct debit to Barnet Area Health Authority for the sum he would have had to pay under the scheme. He said the mailshot which offered a 15% discount for AA members tried to scare people that decent health care was only available for those who could afford it. "I know there are long waiting lists, but the most urgent treatment is generally available...I obviously want good health care for myself and my children, but this is best achieved by working for good health care for all. If richer people exploit the system by paying to move up the ladder then it is going to make things much worse for the poor. I am hoping lots of other people will take this line. We should not be creating a selfish society." Dr Francome has warned the AA he will cancel his membership if he receives any more publicity for its scheme'.

In a letter to me the AA said it was in fact a supporter of the NHS.

In December 1983 *The Observer* reported that private health care bills, which have driven countless Americans to bankruptcy, had claimed their first British victim. John Mitchell was seriously ill with acute inflammation of the brain and was treated at London's Wellington Hospital. He had health insurance but it only covered a small proportion of the total bill. When the problem was realised, an administrator appeared at his bedside and demanded £6,000, which he paid. Then, however, other hospital bills came in and Mr Mitchell lost his job so was unable pay. One of the nursing agencies to whom he owed money took him to court and obtained an order forcing him to sell his flat. He then committed suicide and his cousin commented ' *His death was the direct result of these bills coming in, one after the other, when he had been more or less cleaned out by the first hospital '*.

Any attempts to introduce more financial factors into health care will also be likely to introduce a host of problems.

HEALTH PROBLEMS COMMON TO BRITAIN AND THE UNITED STATES

One common problem is that young house doctors are overworked. In both Britain and the United States, the medical élite have devised a system whereby the youngest doctors in training work extraordinarily long hours for very little money. This period may be compared to primitive initiation rites or to the role of army service in some countries. People are put through the mill to see if they can survive. In 1988, figures showed that 75% of junior hospital doctors worked more than 76 hours a week, and 15% worked more than 100 hours. They also indicated that an eighty hour weekend is common. In this case, a doctor is on call from 9 am Friday until 5 pm Monday. Dr Wendy Savage tells a story of one of her contemporaries who was in a neurosurgical house job and went to Mass one Sunday morning. When the consultant came in he asked for his house surgeon who was summoned from Mass and told: 'Whilst you are my house surgeon you will not attend Mass and I'm sure God will understand'.

One doctor — Simon Durnford, a specialist in aviation medicine — compared the demands on doctors and pilots and said that tiredness was probably a factor in many medical accidents. 'A wrong decimal point, a forgotten drug interaction, or incorrect labelling of right or left and the results may be catastrophic'. Dr David Orton commented 'It strikes us as amazing that there is legislation restricting what coach drivers and pilots do, but not what doctors do'. Dr Garth Hill of the Medical Defence Union said that it was difficult to quantify the effects but that there was plenty of anecdotal evidence. The following three cases will illustrate the problem.

In one case handled by the Medical Defence Union, the doctor's defence society, a doctor who had been on duty 43 hours was called at 4 am to see a baby who needed an injection of salt solution. Instead of sodium chloride the doctor injected potassium chloride having misread the label and the baby died of heart failure.

Two elderly men needed cataract operations, one on the right eye and one on the left. The doctor responsible for the operating list, who had been working all the previous night, mixed them up. One of the patients had a lens removed from his good eye before the mistake was discovered and was left nearly blind.

An anaesthetist, who had been on duty for 36 hours, was telephoned in his hospital room to give an epidural to a woman in labour but fell asleep without replacing the receiver. Two hours later the woman needed an urgent Caesarean but the anaesthetist could not be contacted because his telephone was off the hook and the baby died.

In the United States there has been pressure against such long hours of working. New regulations came into force in New York in 1988 limiting doctors in accident and emergency departments to no more than 12 hours duty at a stretch. From July 1989 junior doctors in all hospital departments were limited to 80 hours work a week with no more than 24 hours without a break. This change follows a campaign by Sidney Zion, a lawyer whose eighteen year-old daughter died after being given the wrong treatment by two emergency doctors who had been working continuously for 18 hours.

HEALTH

Conclusion

There are important changes which, if implemented, would help both Britain and the United States move up the international league table of health indicators.

The evidence shows that those such as Illich, who argue that modern medicine has done more harm than good, are greatly overstating their case. However, it is clear that some things are done which ought not to be done and other things are not done when they should be done.

Some suggestions for change are as follows:

In all the developed countries improvements can be made to the lifestyle which will improve health. Due consideration should be given to environmental effects such as the effect of less fat, no pesticide residues in food and the importance of exercise and the reduction of tension in people's lives. Also important is the benefit of encouraging public transport instead of private cars.

The reduction of poverty and homelessness will help the health of vulnerable groups. There is also a strong case for the medical profession to take a more benevolent view towards alternative medicines and to consider integrating more of the treatments within the overall body of medicine.

There are also relevant differences between countries to consider and the following proposals are relevant.

BRITAIN

- The NHS should maintain its principle of equal treatment to all irrespective of ability to pay.

- The structure of the medical service should be overhauled with an improvement in the position of nursing staff, house physicians and registrars. There should be no cases of doctors suffering from fatigue after working eighty hours in a week.

- Wherever possible, there should be continuity of care. It is particularly important that changes should occur in the care of childbirth where currently, women are often delivered by a maternity team they have not met previously.

- There is evidence that in some medical areas, eg. kidney disease, more resources could be used wisely to prevent unnecessary deaths. People who would be able obtain treatment in the United States may not be able to in Britain. British people are willing to forego tax cuts in order to facilitate improvements in health. A reduction in unnecessary operations such as Caesareans will also help free resources. The percentage of income spent on health is well below that of comparable European nations. So improved health expenditure is a political possibility.

UNITED STATES

- The country clearly under-performs in terms of health indicators. Improvements would follow from the introduction of a comprehensive system of health insurance in the US. There should be a gradual movement away from a fee-for-service system towards one based on capitation. This would reduce the number of unnecessary operations and eliminate financial considerations from the doctor/patient relationship,

- Introduction of no-fault compensation for birth injuries would reduce the incidence of defensive medicine. Development of the trend towards giving midwives more role in deliveries would reflect a change that has been recently introduced in Long Island.

- Changes in environmental factors should be introduced. Weapons control and government support for public transport will help reduce accidental deaths and murders.

- There should be a fundamental re-evaluation of the drug culture surrounding health.

CHAPTER 5

HOW TO REDUCE CRIME

Crime in western countries is at very high levels with many more offences than there were twenty or thirty years ago. In 1951 in Britain there were 1,255 serious crimes per 100,000 population. This has increased to 4,833 per thousand by 1979 and by 1986 had further risen to 7,355. So it has increased nearly six-fold over this period. In the United States the Federal Bureau of Investigation reported that the crime index tripled between 1960 and 1980. It fell 15% by 1984 but then began to rise again.

The high level of crime is of great concern to those of us who care about the environment. Many people are too scared to walk the streets or through parks — this is a great loss to the community and the quality of social life is greatly diminished. Many parents are frightened to let their children walk home on their own from school or local events and instead have to collect them. Due to the concern with robbery and burglary, a great deal of time is wasted locking things up and money spent on anti-theft devices such as burglar or car alarms which often go off accidentally. It follows that a low crime rate would allow society greater freedom and independence.

The increase in crime would have surprised many theorists living in the 1950's. For they largely saw it as something that was due to poverty. So with the growth of wealth, a reduction in crime would be expected as people would not, for example, have to steal to ensure that their children enjoyed the necessities of life. This has not happened and crime levels have risen to much higher rates than in the immediate post-war years. In Britain they have risen twice as fast during the years of Conservative rule than under Labour governments. Crime under Conservative administrations has increased by 7.2% as against 3.6% under Labour. However, neither party can really boast a good record. Indeed one of the ironies of the Thatcher period as Premier is that her government came to power on a strong Law and Order ticket and yet has presided over greatly increased crime rates and very high numbers of people in gaol. So much so that Britain has a higher proportion of its population in prison than any other Common Market country. We have two and a half times the number of prisoners per head of the population as Holland. In the United States too, crime has grown despite successive Presidents believing that high levels of punishment would reduce the incidence of crime.

GROWTH OF VIOLENCE IN THE UNITED STATES

In one year, handguns were used to murder eight people in Britain, thirty-five in Japan, seven in Sweden and 9,014 in the United States. What is more, the problem seems to be growing worse. In the United States, violent crime almost quadrupled between 1960 and 1986 to 617 per 100,000 population — the highest level ever. *The Chicago Tribune* described the first day of 1987. It said midnight on New Year's Eve is not the time to be on the streets for the hidden arsenals of the city are let loose and explode in a furious finale. '*A continuous roar of gunfire rises from some of Chicago's roughest neighborhoods where many of the residents and the police have only one recourse — to duck.*' It continued to quote a police officer '*This is the night when everyone with a gun shoots it off and down here there are a million guns.*' Another said they often have a competition to find out which officer could make the first gun arrest of the year. There are 250,000 registered guns and about 12,000 more are confiscated each year. Between 1965 and the end of 1987 a total of 10,575 people had been killed by guns in Chicago.

In New York the murder rate rose by 5.7% in 1987 to a total of 1,672. This contrasts to a figure of 637 per year for the whole of England and Wales. One report suggested that New York was currently suffering from 'disorganised crime' as the Chinese gangs began to take over power from the Mafia. It seems that one of the reasons for the increase in crime is the growth in cocaine. In November 1988 the *New York Times* reported that Jamaican gangs called 'posses' were some of the most vicious criminals in the United States and had been responsible for 1,400 drug-related killings in the previous three years.There are vast profits to be made. The British *Sunday Times* in February 1989 quoted one man as saying that he made up to $100,000 a week from an investment of $13,000 but that when a gang of Jamaicans moved in on his territory he backed out of the

98

drugs scene. *'They seem to be fascinated with guns. I saw I was going to have to become a cold-blooded killer just to stay in the game . . . so I got out.'* He went on to say that his wife, a university graduate, was a crack addict so when he gave up she took their three year-old and stole $50,000 from him. When he found her a month later she had left the child in a crack house and was working in an abandoned building selling herself for whatever she could get.

Although there is a great deal of violence in parts of New York and Chicago, the latest figures for the highest number of serious crimes per head were in Washington DC, Fort Worth, Texas and Tampa, Florida.

One of the biggest problems in recent years has been the increase in firepower amongst the criminals. In a major article in June 1988 the *Atlanta Journal* talked of the fact that the United States was in a process of entering a second arms race. This time, however, it is an arms race within the United States. It suggested that a weapons gap exists. The criminals, and especially the drug dealers, obtain big money and can buy whatever guns they need to do the job even to the extent of obtaining sub-machine guns that fire 1,000 shots a minute. It added that the police want parity and obtained comments from police forces in difference places. In Los Angeles they said *'We're being outgunned on the streets.'* In Dallas the police said *'When we confront the drug dealers they are better armed than we are.'* In Michigan they said *'Our troopers are willing to take on anyone. All that we are asking is that we can compete on an even footing.'* In Miami the police said *'It's started to get a little ludicrous that the most under-armed people out there are the police officers.'*

The pressure for more firepower grew and since April 1988, Federal agents have been allowed to carry sub-machine guns. Others used semi-automatics which can fire up to 20 shots *'as fast as you can pull the trigger.'* As far as the regular police were concerned there was a move away from the revolver and towards semi-automatic weapons. In 1988 it was estimated that 15-25% of police guns were semi-automatic, but Smith and Wesson reported that orders were pouring in and the percentage of semi-automatics were predicted to increase to 65% by 1993.

In Britain, Jock Young has pointed out that while there is less violence than in the US cities, one half of all households suffer a serious crime every year and 40% of women are virtually curfewed in their houses out of fear.

RAPE IN BRITAIN AND THE UNITED STATES

In 1989, New York was shocked by the attack in Central Park on a 28 year-old white woman jogger by a large group of 30 or 40 black and

Hispanic youngsters in their early teens. She was stripped, beaten, stabbed and raped many times before being left for dead. The eight accused said they were out 'wilding' — a term which comes from the popular rap song 'The Wild Thing' and describes a teenage sexual encounter. They were supposedly part of a vigilante group out to drive crack (cocaine) dealers from the park. The reason the mob attacked the woman appears to have been because she was alone rather than the fact that she was white. When they were initially arrested, the young men treated the episode in a light hearted manner. The event appalled the city despite the fact that there had been 2,000 murders in the previous twelve months. The media called the crime 'the Lord of the Flies' rape because of the youth of the perpetrators and this was one factor in the great concern about the case. The fact is that these youths were brought up in the Seventies and Eighties and showed a disregard for any civilised standards. It clearly raises a great number of questions about the kind of education and family life these young men received.

This incident was also part of a trend. The rates of rape, as measured by Crime known to the Police in the United States, increased four times between 1960 and 1986. Rates of rape are now eight times as high as those in Britain. However, the British problem is getting much worse and during the period 1977-1987 rape was the fastest growing crime. In 1986 the United States had 37.5 rapes per 100,000 of the population compared to four and a half in Britain. Some countries have much lower rates. The Japanese, for example, record only a third as many rapes per head as the British. Later in this chapter I analyse the reasons for this fact, its implications for male sexuality and make suggestions as to the social changes that are needed in order to reduce the number.

One point to bear in mind is that the official figures are a gross underestimate of the number of rapes. Researchers estimate that only about one in five are reported and I would be inclined to put the figure lower than this. I have known six women who were raped and one of these was working on a drugs project in Washington DC and was raped twice in a short period of time. The second occasion happened in broad daylight and she did not tell anyone — not even the man she married — for over five years. I would suggest a reportage rate of about one in eight in Britain, and a lower figure in the United States, maybe one in twelve. Two reasons for the lower reportage rate in the United States are, first, that many of the rapes occur amongst women in minority groups who are very often alienated from the police. Secondly, the clear up rate for rape in the United States is only just over half of those known compared to nearly four out of five in Britain. Going to court can be a very harrowing experience for the victims of rape and very often their evidence is not believed.

A British doctor gained wide publicity in November 1988 when he claimed that one in three allegations of rape is false. Dr Gillian Mezey of the Maudsley Hospital commented that the remark had undermined the attempts of psychiatrists and volunteers working with women to convince them that it was worthwhile reporting attacks and that their claims would be believed. She drew attention to a New York study which found the rate of false allegations to be only two per cent which is comparable to unfounded complaints to the police in other criminal offences.

Rape and other violent acts against women is a great problem in today's society. A study in the Islington area of London published in 1987 found that in terms of non-sexual assault, women were 40% more likely to be attacked than men and that one woman in five knew someone who had been attacked in the previous twelve months. This was despite the fact that women took many more precautions than men. They were, for example, five times more likely to never go out after dark, three times as likely to avoid certain people or streets, and significantly, six times more likely to always go out accompanied rather than alone.

In the United States, the national data show that two in five women do not feel it is safe to go walking in most places at night. The advice from the police is to be careful about their movements. Nassau County police proposed: *'Don't hitchhike, avoid deserted areas. Don't walk close to buildings, alleyways or shrubs, walk aggressively, walk near curbs and in lighted areas, avoid shortcuts, carry keys between your fingers ready to use them, travel with a companion and if you feel you are being followed run for it.'* Women in cars were advised to always check the back seat before entering, not to pick up hitchhikers, if followed to lean on the horn and drive to a populated area, keep doors and windows locked while parking or driving, park in well lit areas, if the tyre bursts, ride on it. If the car breaks down the advice is not to get out — the woman should lock the doors, display a white cloth and ask whoever stops to call the police. This kind of information, of course, implies a siege mentality and has dangers in that any woman who does not carry out all these precautions is likely to be blamed as being foolhardy, even if she is only exercising her right to do things for herself such as mend her own tyre. So this kind of information can lead to the victim taking the blame and also to women being placed in very traditional subordinate roles.

In Britain, young white females are twenty- nine times more likely to be assaulted than those over the age of 45 and thirty times as likely to be sexually attacked. In the United States the latest (1986) data shows a similar pattern, women aged 16-19 are more than thirty times as likely to be raped as those over the age of thirty- five and black women are twice as likely to be raped as white women. In part this latter figure may be reflection of poverty as women with incomes under $7,000 are fifteen times as likely to be raped as those with incomes over $50,000 a year.

A crucial question from these facts is why crime and violence has increased in both Britain and the United States, despite the fact that there are sufficient material needs and that people could live their lives without it? Furthermore what can be done to reduce levels of crime?

THREE APPROACHES TO CRIME

The 'Make my Day' theory of crime

The right-wing theory of crime, with its emphasis on catching and punishing criminals, gains a great deal of support from typical cowboy stories or detective plots with actors like Clint Eastwood in the lead. There are a number of assumptions made in this approach. The first is that there are shared values. That most people are upstanding citizens who abhor crime and want it eliminated. However, there is a small number of people who, through greed, lust or because of a violent streak, break the laws of society. These people need to be punished to teach them the error of their ways and to encourage them to be law abiding in the future. The right-wing believe murderers need to be executed to help rid the world of evil characters, to make the relatives of the victims feel better and to show others tempted to commit such crime to beware. Right-wing politicians often speak of adolescent treatment centres as providing a 'short sharp shock'. It is hoped this experience will ensure that young law breakers will see the error of their ways and become model members of society. There is also a belief that the evidence of this punishment will act as a deterrent to other people and discourage them from turning to crime.

However, one of the problems I see with this approach, and the diet of crime films and such programmes as 'America's Most Wanted', is that it gives a false idea as to how to reduce crime. It implies that the way ahead would be to arm the police force to give them the means to destroy the criminals, and that you need well-armed, disciplined security forces and strong laws to deter crime. The idea put forward is that criminals have done evil things and deserve their just deserts. If they were to escape with wrong-doing completely or with minor punishment, then it would threaten the social order by encouraging others to break the law. In the United States the National Opinion Research Centre has regularly asked people 'In general, do you think the courts in this area deal too harshly or not harshly enough with criminals'. The results have shown an amazing consistency. Each year about 3% of people believe the courts are too harsh while over four out of five say they are not harsh enough. The rest answer the laws are 'about right' or 'don't know'. In fact, American courts are much more harsh than their European counterparts and the proportion of the population in prison is much higher. The reason for the high poll result is that the average person is not yet educated about the limitations of simple deterrence as a means of reducing crime.

It is, however, only one side of the story. It is unfortunate that most people do not understand the causes of crime and believe simply that criminals are people who are selfish, violent and need to be punished.

The view of crime as portrayed in the media makes it very difficult for politicians to do anything other than take the line of *catch the criminals and punish them hard*. In the 1988 US Presidential elections, one of the reasons why George Bush won was that he was able to portray his rival Dukakis as 'soft on crime'. Dukakis responded by taking a tough stance while not, for example, giving in to support for capital punishment. The only solution to this problem is to have a population that is much more knowledgeable than at present.

As far as right-wing criminologists are concerned, their approach is strongly characterised by an emphasis on the individual committing crimes rather than location offences as part of the social structure. They regard the problem of crime to be due to a number of factors. One is the failure of severe enough punishment and the lack of enough police officers to catch the criminals. A second is the failure of liberal and permissive parents to take responsibility for the teaching of proper social rules. In addition, the growth of one-parent families has meant the carer does not have time to discipline the child properly. Some of the Right similarly argue that the increase in women working has led to crime because in the words of one theorist there has been a *'destruction of the nest'*. No-one is at home for a large portion of the day. This, they argue, make the homes less attractive for the adolescent members of the family and yet more inviting to strangers interested only in its contents. The Right believe these factors lead to the spread of what could be called a delinquent syndrome, *a conglomeration of behaviour, speech, appearance and attitudes, a frightening ugliness and hostility which pervades human interaction.*

One idea behind this approach is that many young people do not know the value of right and wrong and that this should be impressed upon them. The right-wing also believe that crime is in a large part, due to the actions of minority groups or immigrants who have not been properly socialised into the values of the society.

A leading United States right-wing criminologist, James Q Wilson, was commissioned by the Institute for Contemporary Studies in 1982 to gather together a number of experts to analyse the crime problem and propose solutions. He also chaired the working party on the control of crime set up by the President and made a number of suggestions. He proposed a more interventionist role for the police. That they should, for example, begin to convict people for drunkenness so as to preserve the order of a neighbourhood, and, in due course, its crime rate. The restraints on police should be removed and, for example, all relevant evidence should be allowed in court even if gained improperly. Any breach of the laws by the police should be dealt with separately. Those arrested should have their records searched by computer for any previous crimes both as a juvenile and an adult, and also be urine tested for drugs. In the community, high risk offenders should be identified and arrested, even if, in a specific instance, they had only committed a relatively minor offence. He proposed more prisons could be built to overcome the lack of space. If dangerous criminals were kept in for long periods, others could be given shorter sentences or supervised in the community.

James Q Wilson also argued that the true aim of anti-heroin laws is to reduce the recruitment of new addicts by making the drug expensive and hard to find, and to encourage the users to seek out programmes which should be readily available. However, he pointed out that a problem with this approach is that it will lead to a higher crime rate among confirmed addicts not interested in treatment as they will rob and steal to support their habit. So Wilson recognised that a tough approach may lead to an increase in crime.

However, in general, the right-wing approach to crime is based on strong punishment which it hopes will reform and deter.

ROBIN HOOD THEORY OF CRIME

The idea that it is good to steal from the rich to give to the poor differs greatly in its assumptions from that of the right-wing 'Make my Day' approach. One of its main points is that the social order is basically unfair. The wealth is disproportionately distributed with the ruling class, who probably have never had to work, but nevertheless have more wealth than the poorer groups to whom life is a struggle. In a situation where the poor are starving, someone who could rob the rich to give the deprived money to buy food would be performing a social service. It would mean that money was transferred away from buying luxuries for the rich towards necessities for the poor.

When I was at the London School of Economics, a Marxist student argued strongly that there was too much inequality in Britain and criminals who robbed the rich were helping to redistribute wealth. This, however, is a doubtful proposition. One point to be made is that some criminals just manage to be half a Robin Hood. They rob from the rich and keep it. As for the rest, research indicated that the poor more often rob their fellow poor than the rich. However, to get a balanced view of crime it is necessary to understand the extreme left-wing position. In 1973 a book was published called *The New Criminology* which set out to show that crime was present, not because of individuals who did not keep to the shared set of values, rather because the social order was at fault. It argued that 96% of crimes were crimes against property, so by abolishing the current system, the large bulk of crime would disappear.

According to this radical left-wing theory of crime, some people are born to riches and others are born poor and this is unfair. Right-wingers like Margaret Thatcher would dispute this, saying that rich children have had parents who have worked hard to provide for their future generations. To the radical Left, one of the purposes of the education and legal system is to try and legitimise the inequalities that exist. So, for example, the ruling class tries to convince people that those who hold élite positions deserve to be there. The legal system is part of the arm of the state to keep the working class in order. The extreme Left have a very negative view of the police, whom they regard as members of the working class who have betrayed their origins and 'gone over' to serve the interests of the rulers.

They point out the ruling class own the media and argue it gives out false ideas to try and prevent people from seeing the inequity of society. It publicises the crimes of the poor but remains quiet about the crimes of the rich and powerful. The Left argues that it is possible to create a different kind of society where property would take on a different nature. People would not be socialised into the belief that ownership is all important. Much more significant would be people's desire to be what they want to be and develop their relationships. Property crime, as we now know it, would therefore disappear.

Violent crime also would be almost non-existent. The new society would be free of the tensions of capitalist societies for many reasons. The so-called 'rat race' — where people struggle to reach the élite positions — would be eliminated.

In the ideal society of the far Left, people would not live in the nuclear family but in larger groupings more like communes. They argue that nowadays many murders take place within the nuclear family. As this would not exist under a more communal society, this type of crime would also cease to exist.

The extreme left-wing view is worth considering because, amongst other things, it identifies the fact that crime is not just an individual phenomena but is due to social causes. It also points us in the right direction in that a change away from the aggressive and self-seeking aspects of capitalism would have an important effect in reducing crime.

There is a car bumper sticker in the United States which says '*God, guns and guts are what made America great, lets keep all three.*' The far Left would argue that there are alternatives to a society which has large numbers of guns and consequently a high number of accidental shootings and murders. Indeed, we do not have to share all its ideas to recognise that many societies have crime rates well below that of the United States and the advantages to society if people could walk the streets in the dark without fear of being attacked.

REALIST APPROACH TO CRIME

This approach at its best bridges the previous two approaches. It both recognises that the social order is unfair and that some offences are committed in desperation due to poverty. However, it identifies crime as a major problem which has a disorganising affect on society. The realists are committed to detailed empirical investigation of crime, recognising the fact that society does need protection and looks to the possibility of measures to reduce the number of offences. Realist criminology is rightly very concerned with street crime because it serves to fragment social relations, undermines security and restricts the individual's movements.

It also recognises the social nature of crime. In Britain, a labourer is fourteen times as likely to go to prison as a professional person; someone aged between twenty and twenty-four is sixteen times as likely to be imprisoned as a sixty-five year old. This kind of analysis shows that some people are in prison because of their position in the social structure. A baby boy is around twenty times as likely to spend time in prison at some time in his life as a girl. This suggests that if society allowed men a different role — perhaps more like women in behaviour — and changed the social conditioning that encourages men to believe that violence is the way to achieve their aims, then the prison population could be less than a tenth its current level.

Furthermore it suggests that prisoners need to be treated in as humane way as possible within the bounds of maintaining order in the society. The realist approach differs from the left-wing Robin Hood approach in a number of ways. For example it recognises some positive aspects of the role of the police in society.

The realist position is better than the right-wing approach for a number of reasons. It is concerned with less visible forms of crime such as 'white collar' and corporate crime. These issues are frequently ignored by the Right but the actions of the wealthy institutions can cause a great deal of damage. A good example was the reluctance of Ford in the US, to change the design of the Pinto despite the fact that fatalities occurred due to a faulty gas tank. The company calculated that it would cost eleven dollars per car to make it safe.

However, the cost of the estimated 180 burn deaths, 180 serious burn injuries and 2,100 burned out vehicles (each death counted as 200,000 dollars) was around 50 million dollars while the recall would have amounted to $137 million. In 1978 a jury in California awarded 127.8 million dollars including 125 million in punitive damages to a teenager badly burned when his Pinto burst into flames.

The realist position also rightly recognises the role deprivation plays in crime. We need to eliminate poverty in order to break the cycle of crime due to poverty. We need to be in the position where everyone can enjoy the better things of life even if they are not capable of holding the highest social positions. The realist accepts that the very nature of society means that the élite, through the control of the media and big business, may attempt to cover up the crimes of the powerful and those guilty of white collar crime will go unpunished.

Unlike the left-wing theory, it realises that we live in the here and now, and does not pin its hopes on some possible future change in society which is unlikely ever to occur. It also understands the reality in that the 'Robin Hood' situation rarely exists. A British government financed study found that the poorest social group — the unskilled workers — were twice as likely to be burgled as professionals. In the United States too, the more deprived groups were more likely to be burgled. Those with incomes under $10,000 suffer a third more burglaries than those with incomes over $30,000. They are also more likely to be subject to robbery, crimes of violence and rape although they do suffer much less personal larceny.

The racial dimensions of crime show similar facts. A British Home Office report showed that about half the offenders reported by black victims were black. British criminologist, Roger Matthews, reports that in the United States too, research indicates a high proportion of inter-racial crime particularly violent crime. A Bureau of Justice report showed that only in one in four cases involving a white victim was the offender black, while where the victim was black under a fifth of the offenders were white. In the United States, black people are more than five times as likely to become homicide victims as whites.

The realist criminologists point out that much of the crime in poor areas is a direct result of deprivation and poor upbringing and that crime just exacerbates the situation. Criminals either do not know, or do not care, about the damaging effects of their crimes and so methods of reducing the number of offences are very helpful. Furthermore, many criminals exhibit very materialistic and acquisitive attitudes. They believe the myths of society that possessions bring you happiness to the extent that they are often willing to risk their freedom to acquire them.

I recently went to a neighbourhood watch scheme in my area where we were told ways of making our homes into small fortresses. However, such approaches to crime, although realistic in some ways, in fact cause a great deal of inconvenience and are unlikely to be successful. Jock Young, a realist criminologist, calculated that a person watching from his or her window is likely to witness a burglary only once every forty-two years. Also there is an inherent danger in turning a home into a fortress as recent cases in Britain have shown — people have died in their homes unable to escape from fire due to heavy security doors.

One important area of debate is what to do with convicted criminals. Some have argued for the abolition of prison. From an objective point of view it does seem a waste of the lives of both prisoners and warders that we now find it necessary to lock up so many people. Prisons can do more harm than good to many offenders. It leads to stigmatisation, and also to young offenders mixing with bad company. Radical alternatives such as community care need to be pursued for those who have committed less serious crimes. The public, however, needs to be protected against the habitual criminal and violence. Prisons need to provide support and a strong education programme. However, later in this book, I shall argue that the solution to crime lies outside the prison and punishment system.

GREENING OF CRIME

In this chapter I have set out three different perspectives of crime. Politicians make statements to the newspapers such as *I'm having a war on drugs* or *We're going to have a crackdown on violence.*The right-wing stress the value of deterrence such as capital punishment and have prison sentences to convince people that crime does not pay. At the other extreme, the Left argue that crime will exist until changes are brought about to balance out inequalities in society.

Although the realist approach has the most to offer, we need to go beyond its parameters and look at an environmental approach to crime. The central point of this chapter is that only when fundamental changes are made in society will there be any significant improvement in the current situation. As previously stated, it is of crucial importance that we move away from a selfish, inward-looking society and towards a more caring, outward-looking attitude. If we can alter society so that people are more concerned with what they can contribute to the world, rather than what they can get out of it, then we will see a large scale reduction in crime. This will be a natural development — not because of fear of punishment as the extreme Right believe, but because if society develops a bias towards making a contribution for the good of humanity, there will be less desire to rob and steal.

WHY RIGHT-WING POLICIES LEAD TO CRIME

All the indicators show that in the United States, crime rates are considerably higher than those of comparable countries. There are a number of reasons for this, and by learning from America's mistakes we will be able to recommend ways of reducing crime.

The first reason is the high amount of poverty. To a really impoverished person, prison can actually be an attractive alternative to his or her current position. There are many people in New York, and growing numbers in London, who are living on the streets. For these people, prison may well not be a punishment but a welcome respite from the vagaries of the weather. If a society has a well developed social security system then even those with social problems — alcoholics, schizophrenics, drug addicts and the disabled will be well cared for. However, if as in the United States, all forms of state expenditure (apart from weapons) are considered suspect, then there will always be pressure to cut out the programmes for the needy and leave them to their own devices or rely on their families to look after them. This can easily lead to more severe social problems in the long term. It also produces a breakdown in a shared culture which in itself acts as a strong deterrent to crime. Poverty, deprivation and crime will be reduced in a society that cares for its members.

The problem that right-wing societies face is their concern that if they give help to all the poor then some of the 'undeserving poor' will also get assistance. The Right, therefore, have to try and target their help with all the inconvenience of means testing and other investigations. This in turn creates an underclass, who, for example, can only earn more money if they work for cash in hand or in twilight occupations. A cycle of poverty is set up with a pool of young people who grow up alienated from society and who are more likely to be involved with a whole range of anti-social activities.

In Britain, the long tenure of a right-wing government is storing up problems for the future. The Schizophrenia Society has pointed out that many sufferers from this illness have been ejected from hospitals and are now in prison. In April 1988, the Government reduced benefits payments to many of the long-term poor and in February 1989, *The Independent* showed how social security cuts had reduced the incomes of kidney disease and cancer patients in Britain. One man who was too ill to work because of chronic renal failure would have received £96 a week but, as he fell ill after the reductions, only receives £63. His family have £83 a week to pay in regular outgoings. A social worker who deals with kidney patients was quoted as saying that before the changes they could always help people but '*Now there are no magic rabbits to pull out of the hat*'. This family, and others like it, will have to adapt to survive and will suffer relative deprivation as

109

their income falls behind that of others. Such policies of creating deprivation are leading to the alienation of a section of the community and the likelihood of the setting up of a crime sub-culture.

There are many such families where children are raised in extreme poverty. We have seen that already crime has doubled since the Tories took office and by taking into account the reduction in the number of teenagers who commit a high percentage of offences, the true increase has been much greater. However, the Government has continued to try and worsen the position of the poorer groups in society. It believes that by increasing the effects of poverty, it will be creating incentives and encouraging people to work. However, what is being created is a United States-style underclass which is proving a breeding ground for crime.

A second reason for the high levels of crime in the United States and Britain is the fact that possession of goods is held in such high esteem. The pressure is to own and not to be. The continual message from advertisements on our television screens is that without a particular product, life is hardly worth living. The overvaluation of material goods gives a false sense of values. Here there is an important role for the education system in forming a buttress against the continuous barrage from advertisers on the need to buy.

The British government has been engaged in a widespread policy of privatisation which may well lead to an increase in crime. When I went to the United States to teach for the first time in 1977, one of my colleagues told me of a technique he used to avoid phone bills. He had a device attached to his phone so that when it was switched on, the phone company recorded a busy signal for which the caller was not charged. So his children, who were away at college, could call home for free. They would make one ring then stop. He or his wife would then switch on the device and the children would have a free phone call. He suggested that I should have one fitted so that people could call me from England and then not have to pay for the call. I replied that if we all did that it would lead to higher phone bills for everyone. My idea was that by paying our bills, we were all contributing for the maintenance of the system. However, his argument was that the high profits made by Bell telephone went to the rich, and his children were more deserving.

When the British government sold shares in the phone company they did so at such a cheap rate that investors almost doubled their money overnight. The vast majority of the population then ceased being shareholders in the sense that everyone owns a part of each nationalised industry and they saw others making windfall profits. I suggest that American-style attitudes will become more prevalent because of this and crime will increase unless we take action.

WHAT NEEDS TO BE DONE

The Left draw attention to the great inequity in the world and the need to develop a world society free from want. We need to devalue money so it can be seen as the means by which people are able to live their lives not as an end in itself. We want young people to be socialised with ideals. Too often we have been educating our young to be insecure about their role in life and so they become self seeking. We need to go beyond this and create a society where people feel secure in their own lives. This would leave them free to devote their energies to helping others. We should teach the young that they should be concerned about what contribution they can make towards the good of the world.

There are those who will argue that people are generally selfish and that *you can't change human nature*. However, we have seen that different societies, different sexes and different social classes have much different rates of crime. This shows that human nature is by no means fixed and that it is possible to change the process of socialisation so that we have different kinds of people. I would maintain that since the 1970's people in many parts of the world, in particular Britain and the United States, have been following right-wing economic doctrines of self-interest which have had very negative effects on the rest of social life.

Once we have created a basic security for people and money takes on less importance than at present, the quality of life will be increasingly appreciated. People should not look to possessions but to their personality development, their friends and relations and how they can contribute to society in general by working to improve the environment for everybody of all nationalities and creeds.

A crucial way of reducing crime is, therefore, to work towards a different kind of society. However, in order to develop these ideas I propose to look at some areas in more detail. These are the ways to reduce violence, rape and how to deal with non-victim related crimes including drugs.

REDUCING VIOLENCE

A three-pronged attack is needed to reduce violence. First, there is a need for restrictions on possession of weapons and, after an amnesty, stiff penalties for non-compliance and illegal possession. In a major report in *The Observer* six years after Reagan had been shot by a handgun bought for $29 (£19) in Texas, the newspaper reported that about 60% of Americans believe in strict gun control. One of their strongest supporters is the wife of the White House Press Secretary,

James Brady, who suffered brain damage when John Hinkley shot the President. But Congress has even relaxed the law, one reason being the fact that the National Rifle Association gives money to nearly half of its members. Reagan continued to support liberal gun laws, even after being shot himself, saying that Washington DC had strict gun restrictions. It seemed to escape his notice that if Texas had stricter gun controls then Hinkley may not have obtained his gun in the first place. In the United States, three in five of all murders are carried out with guns, compared to only one in eight of the many fewer murders in Britain.

There is of course a clear contrast with what has happened to several Presidents of the United States and what happened to the Queen. The young boy who wanted to shoot her could not buy a gun, no matter how hard he tried. He caused a great stir by shooting an imitation gun at her, but had British laws been similar to those in the United States, she may well have been assassinated.

There is also evidence in the United States that gun controls work. For example in Massachussets, tough laws have cut the gun deaths by half. Nationally in the United States 46% of families had guns or revolvers in their homes. One third said they had them for protection, but most had them for recreation. Another study asked people if they felt having a gun in the home made it a safer or more dangerous place. Over a third said 'more dangerous' compared to three in ten (28%) who said safer. The rest said it made no difference. However, every year there are numerous cases of accidental shootings in the home. In addition there are accidental shootings by police.

Any reduction in the numbers of guns would be welcome. It is time for some states to start using unarmed police for regular work. The handgun control lobby now has a million members and if it can turn its support into laws, it could greatly reduce death rates.

A second point concerns the media. Many have argued the case for a reduction in the amount of sex and violence on television. My obser- vation suggests children see lots of violence and very little sex. How- ever, as far as violence goes, I would certainly like to see much less of it. American expert, Dr Tom Radeckie, reported that the average British child sees 80,000 acts of violence before reaching adulthood and that violent scenes can desensitise people and make them lose their temper. Many of the worst offenders are American programmes (*Today* 4 October 1989). To hold up the ideal man to be like those in the 'A' Team is presenting the wrong image. In Britain and Europe, I see dangers in importing films from the United States in which violence is glorified and the roles of men presented in one dimensional ways. I would like to see 'tea-time' violence for children restricted and for us to be presenting more rounded images of people's personalities. A re- duction of the amount of violence in the media is likely to be reflected in life, especially if we can substitute a different kind of image of masculinity. A third point is that our attitudes towards drugs must radically change. The profits need to be taken away and so the economic motive for crime removed. I shall outline later what should be done when considering crimes not involving victims.

WHY THE DEATH PENALTY IS WRONG

There are many who believe that an increased use of capital punishment will reduce violence. In the United States official data released by the Department of Justice indicates the percentage of people favouring the death penalty for persons convicted of murder rose from 60% in 1975 to 70% in 1987. In Britain, too, there is majority support for capital punishment particularly amongst right-wing politicians. However, among those who have studied the issue, there is very little, if any, support. The death penalty is opposed even by right-wing criminologists who realise that it is not effective. This indicates the need to educate the general population that it is not the answer to reduced violence.

In Britain there is no capital punishment, although nominally it could still be carried out in Northern Ireland and for treason. In the United States, the death penalty was abolished by the Supreme Court in 1972 but the rights of states to impose it were restored in 1976. So far 37 of the 50 states have done so. The only NATO ally of the United States still executing people is Turkey.

The murder rate in Britain more or less remained constant from 1946 to the early 1960's and then began to rise — in fact the steady increase has led to a doubling over the early period. In 1972-76 it was an average of nine per million people and rose to an average of eleven per million in the period 1982-86. In the United States, the murder rate per 100,000 inhabitants doubled between 1960 and 1980. It then dropped over 20% in 1984/5 but has since risen. In 1986 it was 8.6 and seems to be rising. In 1986 it was seven times the murder rate for England and Wales.

Those 70% of United States' citizens in favour of the death penalty were asked to give their main justification for being in support. Two in five said that it would protect society and a further one third said that it would deter others. So more than 75% believed that society would be protected. One in five said it was to punish the murderer and the other five per cent did not know.

People believe that the death penalty reduces the number of murders because potential offenders fear it but the evidence does not support this. In the United States, four years after capital punishment was reintroduced to great publicity, the murder rates reached an all 113 time high. The reason one in five gave for supporting capital punishment is revenge — the old adage 'an eye for an eye'. An extension of this argument is that it will make the victim's family and friends feel better to know that the person had been duly executed and so could not escape, be paroled or do any more damage. After almost every political killing in Britain there are calls for capital punishment for 'terrorists'.

Another reason for the death penalty was presented to me by the staff at Marion, the Illinois prison that has taken over from Alcatraz as the highest security prison in the United States. They said some of the convicts justified their murder of other prisoners because it would save the cost of keeping someone in prison for many years. The staff were also in favour of capital punishment as most of the prisoners were there for life and so there were no sanctions. They wanted capital punishment for the murder of warders.

One can sympathise with the staff of prisons having to look after dangerous people for many years. Some of those in Marion were so violent that they were not allowed to come into contact with anyone at all. However, the arguments against capital punishment are more persuasive. The first point is that it is not a deterrent. In Britain, murder is most often committed by someone who is known to the victim. One half involves the family and a further third involves friends. Only about a fifth involves total strangers. Those murderers who commit crimes of passion are often under the influence of alcohol at the time. Capital punishment will rarely deter in such cases.

In the United States, a landmark study of fourteen juveniles on death row by Dr Dorothy Lewis of New York University found that each of them had suffered serious head wounds as children, eight of these were serious enough for the child to be hospitalised and nine of them showed brain damage. All but two had been brutally beaten, whipped or otherwise physically abused and five had been sodomised by other male relatives. Alcoholism, drug abuse and psychiatric illness were common amongst their families. There is a pattern of deprivation and so it follows that a more sensible way of approaching the problem is not to execute offenders, but rather to relieve the deprivation that turns them into murderers. The comparative statistics show that at least seven out of eight murderers in the US would not have become killers if they had been socialised in countries like Holland or Sweden now, or the Britain of ten years ago.

Those criminals who commit calculated murders do not expect to be caught anyway. On the other hand, there are those who are attracted to the idea of being executed. Gary Gilmore asked to be killed, and in January 1977 in Utah, became the first person executed after the Supreme Court reinstated the death penalty. An even clearer example of problems associated with the death penalty is Charles Walker. He had killed a number of people and escaped from custody. He then asked which was the state in which he was most likely to be executed. When he found out it was Florida he went there and killed three women with little attempt to cover his tracks. He was quoted as saying 'I ain't never shed a tear not for them I killed and not for me'. A psychologist was quoted in the *Chicago Tribune* as saying that for some people, capital punishment can be a form of suicide.

There are those who feel that 'terrorists' should be executed. However, this would by no means lead to them being deterred. They always see themselves as 'freedom fighters' and many of them have shown that they are willing to give up their lives for their cause. When the two men drove a lorryload of explosives into the American barracks in Beirut killing themselves and over two hundred and fifty servicemen, they were carrying out an act in which they clearly fervently believed. President Reagan rightly deplored the violence and the suffering of the relatives and friends of those murdered. However, he also said the guerillas were 'cowards' and on this he was wrong. In fact, the act of driving oneself to a certain death takes a great deal of courage. Similarly, Bobbie Sands and a number of other IRA men in prison starved themselves to death to protest against British policy in Northern Ireland. People with such strong beliefs in their cause are clearly not going to be deterred by capital punishment.

One problem with the death penalty is that it does not treat all citizens fairly. In the United States, a convicted murderer is much more likely to be executed if he is poor, lives in the south and has killed a white person. The United States Supreme Court has publicly accepted a detailed study of 2,000 murders in Georgia in the 1970's. It found that a black man convicted of killing a white was 4.3 times as likely to receive the death penalty as a white who had killed a black.

Another argument against the death penalty is that the wrong person can be executed. On 18th October 1966 Timothy Evans was pardoned and the conviction for murdering his wife was overturned. It did not do him much good, however, for he had been hanged sixteen years earlier. The murder was actually committed by John Christie who had said that he was going to give Evans' wife an illegal abortion.

There have been various other documented cases where mistakes have been made and there is always a problem over mistaken identity. I had personal experience of this the day I was asked by the local police to be in a line up. There were about eight of us. The defendant's lawyer was doubtful whether I, with a moustache, and another man with a beard, should be allowed there as his client was clean shaven. In the end they agreed to our presence — the suspect positioned himself first in the line. There were four witnesses to the robbery of a securicor van in Wembley. Two witnesses chose no-one, the third chose an innocent person. The last man came in and when he saw me he shouted aggressively, *'That's the man, that's the man'*. He shook with venom and pointed his finger in my face.

This personal example leads me be suspicious of identification and with capital punishment, mistakes cannot be rectified. Paul Hamann wrote and produced a programme 'Fourteen Days in May' for the BBC in 1987. He was due to film an execution in Mississippi and was profoundly affected by the experience.

He met Edward Johnson, a twenty-six year-old black man from Walnut Grove, Mississippi. In June 1979 a white woman heard a knock on her door after midnight. When she answered a black man assaulted, but did not rape, her. The local marshall was passing and intervened but was shot and killed. Edward Johnson, then an eighteen year-old high school graduate, had a car breakdown that night in the vicinity of the crime. He made a phone call for repairs and so his presence in the neighbourhood was quickly established. He had no criminal record yet the sheriff went straight to his home, and took him to the woman's house. The woman said he was not the man who attacked her and he was released.

Two days later Edward was taken away by the sheriff. They were supposed to go to the state capital for a lie detector test but Edward claimed he was taken to local woods and threatened. He signed a confession when violence was also threatened to his grandmother who brought him up. He repudiated the confession at the first opportunity. The assaulted woman changed her testimony and he was convicted.

He changed his lawyer just before his execution and the new lawyer was 'horrified' at the way his case had been handled. For example, after his car breakdown, Edward had gone to a pool hall where, at the time of the crime, he was with a black woman. She went to court to testify on his behalf but was told to go home and mind her own business. Edward's lawyers did not try to find the woman or persuade the court to hear her testimony. She was finally found a week after the execution.

Paul Hamann wrote in *The Listener* (12 Nov 1987) that the prison doctor, psychologist, chaplain and many other staff all thought Edward Johnson to be innocent. A year later Hamann returned to Mississippi and found the man who actually carried out the murder and who voluntarily confessed to the crime.

One of the strange things about this story is that Hamann did not go looking for a controversial conviction but was given the first one that was available. It is likely that with the restoration of capital punishment in the United States, each year many innocent people are executed. They suffer from a policy that is ineffective and is the wrong way to tackle the problem of violence.

REDUCING RAPE

If we can determine the causes of rape we can see what action to take to reduce or even eliminate it.

One of the more extreme causitive theories is contained in Susan Brownmillar's book *Against Our Will*. This suggests that rape is a conscious process of intimidation by which all men keep all women in a state of fear. However, her work has been rightly attacked by feminists who have pointed out that it does not allow for the widely differing rates of rape between societies. Barbara Toner in her book *The Facts of Rape* uses anthropological evidence as the starting point, and contrasts the behaviour of two tribes. In one with high rates, there was great hostility between the sexes. On the wedding night the sexual act was of great importance to the future status of both husband and wife. The husband tried to force his wife into a position of subordination by repeated acts of intercourse. She tried to resist to bring shame on the man. A second tribe had a much lower rate of rape and the kind of male personality that would commit the act was unknown to them.

Toner suggests that in Western countries, men on the whole are encouraged to take an attitude towards women more like that of the first tribe with a great deal of aggression. The men are expected to be masterful and assertive while the women should be desirable and conquerable. The *British Journal of Community Care* reported an experiment with rapists in which the word 'woman' was written on the board and Ray Wyre, a probation officer, asked them to shout out the first thing that came into their heads. They called out 'hate. . . bitches . . .fuck them. . .dominating. . .mother. . .prick teasers. . .sly. . . lovely. . .in control. . .bastards'. So the results revealed a great amount of aggression towards women. The rapists were also asked if they agreed with such statements as *'women who say no don't mean no, if a woman comes to your flat she's consenting to sex, women like a bit of force'* and *'if a woman allows you to pet her she can't expect you to stop'*. Wyre was not surprised that they agreed with the statements. However, when he then tested the questions on men in the community he was given similar replies. So he suggested that many men have a distorted view of women.

However, my research indicates that careful analysis of the populations of Britain and the United States does, in fact, show great differences in attitudes between the countries. In addition, analysis of the United States shows wide differences over the country. The US Department of Justice provides data for the rates of rape for each of the states. This shows that the highest rate of rape is in Alaska with 73 rapes per 100,000 population followed by Nevada and Michigan. The lowest rate was in Iowa with a rate of 12 per hundred thousand. *117*

So a woman in Alaska has six times the chance of being raped as one in Iowa.

The differences between Britain and the United States are very instructive. There was some trouble during the last war because American servicemen had very different attitudes towards sex. The well-known American anthropologist, Margaret Mead, wrote a pamphlet called *The American Troops and the British Community*. In it she pointed out that in the American system of courting the boy demanded innumerable favours which the girl gained status by refusing. *'A really succesful date is one in which the boy asks for everything and gets nothing'*. In contrast the British men tended to only press hard for sex if they were serious about the girl and unlike the American men, would feel a sense of responsibility to any women they made love to.

The situation has changed a great deal in the intervening forty-five years but the basic cultural difference remains. In 1978 I published the results of a survey I carried out of a thousand students on Long Island, N. Y. I asked whether they agreed or disagreed with the following statement. *'Boys should not go to bed with someone they have just met, for example, at a party'*. The responses of the replies varied greatly according to sex. Sixty per cent of the young women agreed with the statement compared to only 22 per cent of the men. So the men were only one third as likely to oppose casual sex. In order to see if the men thought it acceptable to have sex themselves but not the women, I asked whether the students agreed with women having casual sex and the vast majority of men did . Less than one in three (31%) were opposed to it. So the vast majority of men were not opposed to casual intercourse for either sex. Again there was a strong difference in replies. The women tended to the view that casual sex was wrong for both sexes.

These attitudes show quite clearly what is going to happen in casual encounters. The man will press for sex and the woman will resist. In Britain, too, there has always been a double standard, but for a number of reasons it is not so strong. One factor amongst the students has been the grant system which means that both sexes have about the same amount of money. There is then no financial reason why the man should normally pay when couples go out, and therefore eliminates the sex horsetrading which often results from such sexist relationships. In my book *Abortion Practice in Britain and the United States,* I looked at the reasons why there were many more unwanted pregnancies in the United States. I found that there were significant differences in contraceptive practice between the countries. British men were much more likely to use birth control than American men, who would often make comments about using condoms such as *'It is like having a shower with your raincoat on'*. They also did not seem as concerned that the women might face an unwanted pregnancy. In fact amongst

American men there is a phrase about keeping women *barefoot and pregnant*. No similar phrase has wide currency in Britain. The British men I interviewed were by no means angels who would protect women, but they had far more concern and interest than their American contemporaries.

Similarly, amongst American women there is often hostility towards the men. One story that was retold by a group of feminists in 1979 was of a biologist who was raped by four men. She did not get angry but asked if they would like to go back to her apartment for coffee. When they did so she slipped drugs into their drinks and while they were asleep she castrated them all. The story does seem a little unlikely. However, it was retold with jubilation and it does indicate a greater division between the sexes than exists in Britain.

I would suggest that this sex difference is one reason why the rates of rape are much higher in the United States. In societies where men are socialised to be active sexually, to be dominant and persuade women to comply it is only one more small step to rape. In these countries, rape can simply be seen as the polar end of normal male/female relationships. So one way to reduce the number of rapes is to work towards a society where, instead of the men being assertive and the women passive, both sexes are free to develop their personalities.

A second factor is the level of violence in society. Rape is always associated with either actual or the threat of violence, so a reduction in the general level of violence in society will have an effect in reducing the number of rapes. This also applies to other crimes. Sometimes burglars will commit rape as part of a robbery. So a decrease in housebreaking would also be likely to lead to fewer sexual attacks.

The final point leads us back to a major theme of this book — that we need to develop a society where people in general care for others. With these kinds of values there would be no thoughts of rape. Instead of thinking only of their own gratification, men would want to help others.

WHERE THE LAW SHOULD NOT BE

The law has on too many occasions, intervened in areas of private morality and in so doing has diverted the attention of the police and other law enforcement officers from other work. Edwin Schur wrote a book with the title *Crimes without Victims*. In it he argued there were a group of crimes in which there was no complainant. The sorts of offences which may come into this category are drug taking, prostitution, under-age drinking, illegal gambling, homosexuality and certain heterosexual acts such as under-age sex, birth control and abortion. Many actions are crimes, not because they do any damage, but *119* because they offend against the moral order and present special difficulties in terms of policing. They lead to police corruption, to arbitrary infractions of the individual's freedom and to greater social problems. In general, I would argue that with due protection of the young and the vulnerable, crimes without victims should be decriminalised.

If we take prostitution for example, it is often illegal and the law has adverse affects. The police can only detect a fraction of what occurs. In the most common case in which men use female prostitutes, they are clearly not going to report themselves. So it is very difficult for the police to obtain information leading to arrest without some kind of entrapment. Also, after a while, police build up a relationship with experienced prostitutes which can well lead to bribery and corruption. The police promise not to make arrests in return for bribes or favours. Prostitution illustrates the conflict between public attitudes in which it is seen as shameful and the private fact that many people use such services.

If we take the example of abortions we can see that over the years they were carried out illegally with only arbitrary police action. In Britain, when abortion was illegal, those breaking the law were often highly respected amongst the women who used the services. In my book *Abortion Freedom* I told of an incident where a woman, Mrs Lee, was prosecuted for carrying out an abortion. The crowd cheered and waved her off to prison. In contrast there was great anger against those responsible for her conviction with shouts of '*come down you dogs*'. I taped an interview with US activist Bill Baird in 1979 who had been imprisoned for giving a can of birth control foam to a young single woman at Boston University. He challenged the law which reached the Supreme Court and resulted in all prohibitions on birth control in the United States being overthrown on the grounds of privacy in 1972. However he was never imprisoned for abortion activism, despite the fact that he was openly arranging terminations. In fact in 1967 a leading black women's magazine had his phone number published on the front cover with an invitation to call if an abortion was required. He told me that two things prevented any action against him. The first was that he made women sign a statement saying:

'I came to Bill Baird voluntarily seeking his abortion help. I am not connected to the Police Department. I was charged no fee and I do not hold him responsible for my actions.'

The second point was that many of the prominent local citizens have used his services and he threatened to release the information if he was arrested. He was not the only one to flout the law. In fact in 1967, the *New York Times* revealed that 21 local Protestant and Jewish clergymen set up a consultation service to refer women for abortion.

These two examples show the difficulty in law enforcement and that the law is probably not the best way to deal with problems in the area of voluntary sexuality except to protect the vulnerable. However, the victimless crime of most concern to us is drugs. The first point to make is that societies have a totally irrational attitude towards them. One of the most addictive drugs and the one which kills most people is tobacco, yet this is legal. Alcohol faces more restrictions and there is a great deal of difference in attitude between Britain and the United States. A national survey in the USA conducted by Gallup found that 80% of people would favour a national law raising the drinking age to twenty-one. Preliminary results of my research into attitudes to drinking indicate that in Britain such a question would not get the support of one in five. For the British, it is the other kinds of drugs such as marijuana, cocaine and heroin which face the most public censure.

There is a great difference between Britain and the United States in attitudes to both marijuana and cocaine. In Britain, both are very much opposed by public opinion, but in the USA attitudes are divided at least towards marijuana.

In 1975 the Supreme Court of the State of Alaska ruled that the consitutional right to privacy protects the possession of marijuana for personal use in the home by an adult. A further ten other states have decriminalised it — California, Colorado, Maine, Minnesota, Mississippi, Nebraska, New York, North Carolina, Ohio and Oregon. In addition, all but seventeen of the states have enacted laws allowing the medical use of marijuana for patients being treated for glaucoma and cancer.

In 1986, only two in five (42%) of high school seniors believed marijuana should be illegal, although if all ages were considered, the majority of the US population thought it should be banned. One interesting statistic is that in 1987, 113 million marijuana plants were destroyed. This is about half a plant for each member of the population.

Marijuana/hashish use has declined amongst high school seniors in the United States. The percentage who had used it within the previous month declined from 27% in 1975 to 23% in 1986. However, a majority of high school seniors had used it at some time.

The situation with cocaine in the United States seems to be very similar to the position of alcohol in the 1920's. The most recent of Michigan University's annual surveys of High School Seniors found that only a third (33%) believed that people risked harming themselves physically or in other ways if they used cocaine once or twice. The price of cocaine has dropped substantially. The Drug Enforcement Administration estimates it fell from $640 a gram in 1977 to $100 a gram in 1987.

The great problem with policing cocaine is that it is a very popular drug amongst the wealthier groups so its very illegality means that *121* there are great profits to be made. The violence associated with it has led to the deaths of many police officers. One in New York came just a few days after the drugs dealers warned the police that they would carry out an assassination if harrassment continued.

There is little doubt it would be better for society if the consumption of drugs was greatly reduced. Over half the inmates in US State prisons were under the influence of drugs or alcohol at the time of their offence and drug abuse leads to numerous social problems. The high percentage of babies born in New York with the Aids virus is due, in large part, to the use of drugs.

However, the question is which is the best approach? President Bush has said that he intends to bomb the crops. Although this may have political benefits for him, its wider effects are more problematical. As mentioned earlier, the Right argues that the aim of anti-drug laws is to reduce the recruitment of new addicts by making drugs expensive and hard to find. It would therefore encourage existing users to seek out treatment programmes. However such laws only lead to crime as addicts rob and steal to support their habit. Also the high profits finance a wealthy criminal subculture.

My suggestion is that the best way to deal with victimless crimes is not to make them illegal, but to use other methods to control them. There is a need to recognise that many people have problems with drugs but that this should not automatically make them criminals. Society should help the drug dependent. For some it will mean treatment programmes even if that means simply maintaining the habit.

In May 1989, an editorial in *The Independent* commented on the level of violence and drug use in the United States. It argued for gun control saying that the United States should have outgrown the idea that *'one is not a full citizen without a pistol in one's belt'*. However, it argued that in the short term, strict gun control laws are not a political possibility. It also said that drugs were a more promising field, that the prohibition of drugs has been no more successful than the prohibition of alcohol. Criminals make millions of pounds while the lives of millions of Americans are blighted. The paper called for the President to nationalise the supply of drugs and make it legal for the states to sell them, so undercutting the bandits who make a fortune out of the trade. It also argued it would help bring the addicts out into the open where they could find treatment. Others have come to similar conclusions. Peter Bourne, who was special assistant to President Carter on US national drug policy, wrote in *The Times* (6 Sept 1989) that the cocaine trade is Colombia's second largest foreign exchange earner and provided employment for over a million people in Latin America. He argued that the increase in violence with what is effectively a US sponsored civil war, will only worsen the level of suffering, death and corruption. It will not end the trade while the US remains a multi-million dollar market for the drug. In addition he pointed out that, while the worldwide deaths from cocaine were less than a thousand, more than two million die from the effects of tobacco. He drew attention to US Vice President Dan Quayle's hypocrisy in attacking some drugs yet demanding the Thai government should open up its society to US cigarette companies or face sanctions.

We can see clear parallels between the current drug crisis and the prohibition era. We cannot eliminate cocaine but we can bring it under control, reduce the violence and corruption associated with it, stop it falling into the hands of the young and in due course, reduce people's need for such artificial stimulation.

CONCLUSION

This chapter shows that much of current policy on crime is based on misinformation and is ill advised. The values of greed preached by successive governments have resulted in too much emphasis on material goods. In addition, the ideas of competition have led to people striving against each other rather than basing their relationships on a spirit of co-operation and help. If we change the goals of society and the values that underpin it towards a more caring world, then we will be creating an environment in which crime will wither at the vine. The degree of misinformation on such issues as the causes of crime and the efficacy of different solutions means there is much to be done in educating the public. Once people accept that capital punishment is not a deterrent and can see through the illogical attitude to drugs perpetrated by some politicians then sensible policies will become political possibilities. The environment will then be much freer from the fear of theft and violence and people will be able to live their lives in a much more relaxed way.

Chapter 6

ONE WORLD, ONE PEOPLE

The evidence already provided in this book shows the misallocation of resources. The fact so many children lack adequate diet, care and opportunities to develop themselves is nothing short of a major scandal. In October 1989, the *New Internationalist* reported that 30 out of every 100 children in Mali, West Africa die before the age of five. This contrasts to one in a hundred in Australia, Canada and the UK and the situation is deteriorating further in many parts of the world. Although the gap between the rich and poor in this kind of statistic had narrowed in the early 1980's, surveys of particular countries in Africa and Latin America show that the numbers of malnourished children are now increasing. This should be high on the political agenda. For many, diet will be so poor that their intellect will not develop properly. Others may suffer unnecessary blindness and other preventable health hazards.

The United States, and Britain in particular, are currently missing many opportunities to help develop a world free from poverty and want — indeed they are hindering such development. Despite the fact they are powerful and wealthy countries, their moral standards could be considered to be lower than many smaller, less developed countries. The United Nations set a target that governments should give 0.7% of their Gross National Product (GNP) in overseas aid. Only four countries meet this target — Holland, Sweden, Denmark and Norway,. Although money is only one element in the needs of poor countries, their levels of debt make it vital. Chris Brazier, writing in the *New Internationalist*, has pointed out that in the Marshall plan, by which the United States helped restore Europe after the Second   *125*

World War, the United States gave 2% of its GNP each year. Today, when the US wealth is two and a half times greater, it gives only 0.22% of its GNP to overseas aid. Furthermore much of this is window dressing and more detailed examination of the 1986 figures shows that a quarter of US aid goes to Israel while the 45 African countries have to share one-fifteenth of the aid package. So the little money available goes to developing strategic interests rather than helping people in need.

Britain is a prime example of a country which has missed a great chance to help others. In the late 1970's the country had the bonus of its great oil reserves being developed and coming on stream. This meant that it was richer than at any time in its history and had the opportunity of developing programmes not only to help its own poor but also to make a greater contribution to the global effort towards ridding the world of poverty once and for all. However, its help to the developing countries declined despite the genuine concern amongst the people of Britain to help others. When Bob Geldof set up Band Aid it raised a great deal of money and many people give on a regular basis. The Princess Royal has travelled around the world promoting the Save the Children Fund and giving information on what needs to be achieved in the future.

Yet the Government has remained largely unmoved and it has been very cynical in its manipulation of public opinion. In 1988 I was with other jugglers at a television studio helping raise money for Africa. Just after we had been interviewed, the Government made an announcement that it would contribute one million pounds towards the fund which at the time stood at twelve million. So the Government appeared on the surface to be very sympathetic to the plight of those in poverty. However I knew that the British government had been steadily cutting help to the poor. In real terms, British help to the poor fell between 1979 and 1987 by 36%. Despite the desperate human crisis and the unprecedented concern of the people to the plight of the poor, Africa suffered a decline of 26.5% in British aid over the eight years. In absolute terms it was cut from £386 million in 1979 to £284 million in 1987 measured at 1989 prices. So the Government quietly cut help to Africa by £102 million and yet amidst the blaze of publicity gave a paultry million back.

Britain remains officially committed to the UN aid target of 0.7% of GNP towards aid. In 1979 it reached 0.52% but by 1987 had fallen to 0.28%. It is not that Britain cannot afford to help, Margaret Thatcher told the House of Commons on 28 February 1989 'We now have a higher standard of living than we have ever known. We have a great budget surplus'. So there is clearly scope for reversing the trend of the past eleven years.

WE WANT NO WARS BUT A WAR ON WANT

There were signs in the 1950's that even Republican politicians were seeing the stupidity of the direction in which the world was going. President Eisenhower for example, rightly commented: *'Every gun that is made, every warship that is launched every rocket fired signifies a theft from those that hunger and are not fed, from those who are cold and not clothed'*.

Yet we hear few such comments these days from the governments of the United States and Britain. The level of armaments is at an all time high. In 1944 when an atom bomb fell on Hiroshima, 118,661 people were killed, 30,524 people were severely injured, 48,606 were slightly injured and 3,677 went missing making a total of 201,468 casualties in all. Many of these died later from the injuries they had sustained. Since that time there has been 'successful' research to make even more powerful bombs. It took a heavy bomber to carry the five ton bomb to Japan. Now the yield of explosive to the weight of the bomb has increased by over 150 times. By 1981 one Poseidon submarine carried sixteen missiles each with ten warheads — each of the warheads had three times the force of the Hiroshima bomb. So each submarine carried four hundred and eighty times the explosive power that hit Hiroshima — more than the total explosive power used by all the munitions in the Second World War.

In the succeeding years this firepower has increased. If all industrialised countries were to increase their overseas aid to the 0.7 per cent level recommended by the UN it would cost an extra $50 billion a year. This seems a large sum but it is only about as equal to expenditure on the military every four weeks.

ROCKET THEORY OF GROWTH

Many economists believe that the world should develop along parallel lines to the economic growth in the West. One idea put forward by Walt Rostow a former American government adviser, was that the underdeveloped countries should pass through five stages before reaching a standard of living comparable to the United States. The first stage is a traditional society, then they should begin to develop the second stage — 'preconditions for take off'. The third stage is 'take off', ie. countries would be producing more goods than required for their immediate needs and could begin to invest substantially. The fourth stage is a 'drive to maturity' until finally they reach the 'age of mass consumption'.

However, there are great problems with this theory. First the energy required is not available and is not likely to be unless there is some amazing technological breakthrough. The United Nations World Commission on Environment and Development pointed out that to bring the developing countries' energy use up to the level of the industrialised countries by the year 2025 would require increasing the present global energy by a factor of five with all the resulting problems of global warming and energy shortages.

Secondly there is the problem of pollution. For example, if all the Chinese were to begin buying refrigerators this would considerably increase the damage to the ozone layer due to the effect of CFC gases. The United States currently emits over three hundred cancer-causing pollutants into the atmosphere. If similar pollution occurred on a worldwide basis, the ecological problems would multiply. Thirdly, the general problems faced by the rich countries raise questions about the desirability of such a development.

RAPE OF THE THIRD WORLD

One of the biggest problems is that the economic system is ordered in such a way that there is a net outflow of wealth from the poor to the rich. This is the case today and has been for many years, as the rules of society were designed to benefit the rich. Between 1950 and 1965, $9.0 billion of investment flowed from the United States to the developing countries while $25.6 billion profit flowed back. In the 1970's many governments were offered loans from Western banks on the basis it would be easy to industrialise and so pay the loans back. However, only a handful of countries like South Korea could do so. Since 1984 grants of aid and new loans have been far outweighed by the amount the poor countries pay back to the rich, currently at least $20 billion a year. At the beginning of 1989 the debt of the Third World countries stood at $1.2 trillion, and many of them have little hope of ever repaying this debt. It has been made more difficult in recent years as the prices the underdeveloped countries could get on the world markets have declined 30% since 1979.

The debts have, in part, developed gradually from the net outflow of capital from the poor countries. However, they have also come from inept projects supported by a corrupt élite. In the Phillipines, the Marcos government paid $2.1 billion for a nuclear power station which never opened partly because it was built in an earthquake zone. Marcos himself received 80,000,000 dollars from Westinghouse as commission for placing the contract. The interest on this loan is half a million dollars a day.

The repayments of the massive debts leads to great problems for the Third World. The International Monetary Fund forces the debtor countries to cut public expenditure, push up the price of food and, instead of serving the needs of their own community, produce cash crops for export. In his book *After the Crash*, Guy Dauncy reports that a Mexican study in 1984 found that half of all households showed calorie and protein deficiency. Another study showed that 70% of lower-income Mexicans could not afford to eat fruit, vegetables, eggs and fish. The debts the country were servicing led, in 1986, to over $2 billion dollars worth of fresh fruit, vegetables and beef being exported to the United States.

The problem of debt needs to be tackled to help rid the world of poverty. The situation is complicated by the fact that in order to repay the debts, the underdeveloped countries may have to take action harmful to the environment. In 1987, the US group, Conservation International bought $650,000 worth of Bolivia's debt in return for an agreement from the Bolivians to preserve four million hectares of precious environmental habitat. This is an area about the size of Wales. The World Wildlife Fund negotiated a similar agreement with Costa Rica and a World Conservation Bank has been set up to collect money for further deals.

This approach could succeed with Brazil. The destruction of the rainforests is causing catastrophic environmental problems. The soil in which they grow is thin and once the trees are felled, the land will only yield crops for about five years before it becomes infertile and turns to hard baked sand. This in turn increases the Earth's desert areas, accelerates the increase in the amount of carbon dioxide released into the atmosphere and disrupts the pattern of rainfall. So if Brazil and other countries such as Indonesia and the Phillipines could be persuaded to trade off some of their debt for the preservation of their natural areas, the benefits would be felt worldwide. We must look to a change in attitude amongst people and governments in the rich countries to finance such schemes.

DISTORTION OF THE MARKETS

In Chapter Two I outlined the problems for developing countries of childhood illness caused by the selling of powdered milk. Medical drugs are another problem area. In the world economy, drugs are treated as a commodity to be sold at great profit. Their abuse can harm many people. In Bangladesh in 1982, the government's expert committee on drugs estimated that a third of the money was spent on totally useless tonics and other medicines considered inessential by the World Health Organisation.

Another problem is that drugs that are banned or severely restricted in developed countries are often freely available over the counter in the Third World. Anabolic steroids are used in developed countries medically for serious degenerative bone diseases, severe anaemia and some forms of cancer. The Dutch company, Organon, has been selling steroids under the name Orabolin to children claiming that the preparation will aid optimum growth. However, side effects are known to cause liver tumours and irreversible masculinisation of females. The Lancet (7 Oct 1989) reported that two development action groups in Switzerland, which had earlier played a leading part in a campaign against Nestlé's advertising of baby milk, presented an assessment of the medicines Swiss companies sent to the Third World.

Half (48%) of the drugs are considered inappropriate and only 17% are included in the WHO model list of essential drugs. Almost one in five are categorised as 'nonsense' preparations and some of these are dangerous. Many of the drugs were no longer sold in Switzerland and the groups called for laws to control export 'What we don't want to tolerate in our country, we cannot tolerate on the soil of others'.

OPPONENTS OF AID

Two professors at the London School of Economics, Peter Bauer and B S Yamey, argue that, despite good intentions, much of the aid given to underdeveloped countries has in fact been counterproductive. They argue that Third World policies have been too biased towards the urban areas and that aid has all too often been used to buttress this élite rather than to benefit the rural poor. Furthermore, they maintain, the aid has been given to governments rather than directly to the poor themselves. They ask for example 'How do the poor in Pakistan and Nigeria benefit from the creation of new capital cities'. They also point to the fact that aid has gone routinely to Third World countries at war with each other such as India and Pakistan, to Cuba when it was maintaining troops in Africa and to countries which are openly hostile to the West.

Many of these points are sound, but what Bauer and Yamey neglect to point out is that one reason why much of the aid in the past has not been effective is not simply that is was misdirected. It was sent primarily not to help the poor but to keep governments friendly. It was more an instrument of foreign policy than a help to the poor.

THE WAY AHEAD

What is needed is a three-pronged programme to help transform the social and economic climate of the world. The first is a major reduction in the expenditure on armaments, secondly, new policies towards development and thirdly, an attack on the problem of over-population and unwanted children.

On the first issue we can see dramatic improvements even in the past few years. I have several cuttings from the early 1980's with headlines such as 'Communism evil focus in modern world says Reagan'. He saw a necessity to improve the United States' armed forces for *'America to be able to walk tall again'*. During his era, there was an unprecedented rise in expenditure on armaments and unwarranted interference in affairs around the world. Between 1984 and 1987 the United States defence expenditure grew by 57 billion dollars to a sum of 288 billion dollars. This increase is greater than *total* expenditure in 1987 for the United Kingdom, Belgium, Canada, Denmark, Greece, Portugal, Turkey and Norway all added together. All these countries' expenditure added together came to 56 billion dollars. It is clear that the United States intends to reduce arms expenditure, however, levels are likely to remain dangerously high. Despite the changes in Eastern Europe, the US still views many countries as potential enemies and the size of the army depends on the degree of perceived threat.

It is now evident that the Soviet leadership has changed. When in 1989, I ran the Moscow Peace Marathon, I found a great desire for peace among the Russian people. They have suffered so much in previous wars. It is a welcome development that the Soviet leadership has come so far in such a short time and moved more in accordance with public opinion. It is time for the British and Americans to stop aiming nuclear bombs at the Soviet Union and look to disarmament. In the world as a whole, at least one in four of all the scientists and engineers in research and development are working on weapons. If we free these people to begin positive production then a great fillip can be given to development.

Since the Second World War, the Japanese have been refused permission to spend more than one per cent of their GNP on armaments. This has meant that, whereas countries like the United States, Britain and the other NATO countries have been wasting their money on weapons which are non-productive, the Japanese have been able to make investments and put their scientists to work researching other products. The country now has a great deal of economic power and wields a greater influence in the world than had it spent its money on armed forces. When Emperor Hirohito was buried in February 1989, 55 Heads of State attended, which is more than observed the funerals of either Presidents Kennedy or Brezhnev.

The United States has maintained the presence of armed forces in different countries in order to retain access to raw materials. One point made by Guy Dauncy is that the United States would benefit more if the money it currently spends on keeping a fleet in the Mediterranean was used to develop energy saving methods at home. It would not only save money but also avoid such accidents as the shooting down of the Iranian airliner and the subsequent retaliation.

So there are a number of reasons why the US maintains a large number of armed forces. However, from this discussion there are good reasons for reducing this number significantly.

The same applies to many of the poorer countries. Data obtained from the Institute of Strategic Studies shows that many countries with serious economic problems are wasting their resources. In 1987, for example, Ethiopia had 320,000 people in its armed forces, more than the United Kingdom. Military expenditure was approaching one fifth of all government expenditure. In Zimbabwe too, almost one fifth of total government expenditure was on the military. Other countries in Africa had among the highest proportions of military expenditure in the world. In Chad in 1986, two thirds of government expenditure was on the military and in Mozambique it was two fifths. Nigeria, however, has cut the size of its armed forces from 133 thousand in 1984 to 95 thousand in 1987 and more than halved the amount of government spending on the military over this period.

The 1987 data shows some variation in Asia. In India and Thailand the military takes a fifth of government expenditure, in Pakistan it is over a third and in Taiwan it is two-fifths. In contrast, in China it is one-eleventh, Malaysia one-twelfth and New Zealand one-twentieth. So there are wide variations and the highly militarised countries have a great deal of scope to transfer their resources to help improve their social conditions.

In general, the evidence indicates that the world is far too militarised. A realistic target would be to reduce expenditure by fifty per cent over five years and direct those resources into a massive fight against poverty.

PEOPLE TO END POVERTY

There is a great need for a change in direction in terms of the help and encouragement that the rich countries give to the poor. Ghandhi once said that the poor of the world cannot be helped by mass production but needs the production of the masses. The techniques used by the labour saving devices of the rich world are usually not appropriate for societies where labour is abundant.

I can remember as a child going on a walk to raise money for tractors for the hungry. The aim was to send tractors to help the poor grow their own food. On the surface it seemed a good idea, but there were inherent problems. The tractor would cost a great deal of money to maintain, it if broke down there might not be anyone available to repair it or the parts might take a long time coming. However, smaller scale equipment could be used by the local people with little or no danger of breakdowns, and would use the local available labour. It was Fritz Schumacher who called this engineering 'Intermediate Technology' and in the late Sixties I attended a demonstration where he showed an egg box production plant in use in Zambia. It was not highly mechanised like those in Western countries but used the labour of local people. This had a great many advantages including the fact that many people were employed in jobs in which they believed.

Many economists in rich countries have assumed that what is best for the rich is also likely to be best for the poor. The leaders of the underdeveloped countries are often educated in countries like Britain. Consequently when they return home they want to develop their societies in a similar manner. This has meant, for most poor countries, a dual economy in which about 15% of the population live in cities while the vast majority live in rural areas. The aid from rich countries is not only too little to make up for current and past exploitation but is also wrongly directed. A few examples will indicate the fact that the money is often not best spent to help those in need. The British government made the Indian government take Westland Helicopters as part of its aid package. This was presumably in order to boost the sales of the troubled organisation. *The New York Times* (20 August 1989) reported that ten years after distributing $40 million in aid for medical equipment in Indonesia, Tokyo discovered that most of it was lying unused because no-one in the Indonesian hospitals knew how to use it. *The Ecologist* in 1986 reported that the Soviet Union provided the money for a tiny village, Madhubassa, at the bottom of the Himalayas, to build a tobacco factory. It lies between two rivers and, as trees were cut down to cure the tobacco, it led to increased flash flooding which eroded the banks of the rivers and threatened the existence of the village. These are good examples of the wrong kind of help.

Aid needs to be of a different kind, and the Intermediate Technology Development Group has been leading the change in direction. Instead of directing effort to help the commercial and political interests of the rich countries, or the rich in the poor countries, a new deal is needed. The exact nature of the help must be related to the needs of the local inhabitants, but some general points can be made about its features.

- Any developments should be based on the skills of the local population, so there will be greater use of the human resources already available.

- Any jobs created should be based in the places where the people live rather than cause great disruption of local communities.

- There should be discussions with the local people about their aspirations and goals, so that any help ties in with their aims and is therefore more effective.

- The workplaces must be cheap enough so that they can be formed in large numbers to employ local people.

- As far as possible, local materials should be used.

- Thought should be given to the long-term ecological effects of the developments with the aim being to improve the environment.

- Information should be shared amongst the developing countries.

The Intermediate Technology Development Group has been developing a variety of techniques since its formation in 1965. Working in partnership with Third World development agencies, it has added to local knowledge by providing technical information and advice in several areas. In the area of food production, it has helped improve animal husbandry techniques, water catchment and irrigation systems and the preservation of fruit and vegetables. In helping rural industries it has improved building materials from locally available resources, produced better machinery for cottage textile production and proposed appropriate processes for small scale mining operations. It has developed simple workshop equipment for use with wood and metal, devised low cost transportation methods for small farms and improved the techniques for building and using fishing boats. In the development of energy systems, it has produced windpumps and other water lifting devices, developed small hydro-electric systems for remote hill villages and helped to introduce fuel efficient domestic cooking stoves.

Some more specific examples are as follows:

★ In Sri Lanka, as in other countries, one of the problems for small scale farmers is that there is a lack of appropriate technologies for preserving and processing what they grow. Food crops are rarely available throughout the year, and so without adequate means to keep and store food, over half of it may have to be thrown away and scarcity can follow surplus. The existing technology has been largely too complicated and expensive so, the Group has been helping people develop low cost techniques for preservation. In Sri Lanka these centre around dehydration and acid preservation which have a low risk of health hazards and can be used by non-specialised groups using unsophisticated equipment. The techniques can be used for a wide range of goods including fruit, vegetables, fish, meat and spices. This also helps people by increasing the value of the crops that can be sold in the local markets.

★ In Kenya, disease often kills chickens. The Group helped set up a system to train Community Animal First Aid Workers. As part of this, eleven women were trained as poultry vaccinators which resulted in the treatment of over 1,500 chickens in a single day.

★ One problem in Ghana is the moving of farm crops and other merchandise to the point of sale rather than by the traditional method of carrying it on the head. In 1989, the first Intermediate Technology Transport Cycles were used in the city of Kumasi. The initiative has been specially adapted for local economic conditions making using of available low cost materials and is sponsored by the World Bank. The trailer's particular advantage over other bicycle-based forms of transportation is a ball and hitch mechanism which allows the trailer to be detached easily when not in use.

★ In the Amazon basin town of 3 de Octubre, the machine used to make peanut butter had no gearing system which made it difficult for the women to use. A new machine reduces the effort required to grind the peanuts by 60 per cent, and is even being used by young children. It incorporates a simple system of gears using a rachet and a bicycle chain and can easily be made in local workshops using readily available materials. Peanut butter production in the community has proved very successful, providing the women with a higher income than they could get from working as labourers on the land. It has the additional advantage of allowing them to stay in their villages where they can retain contact with their children. The success of peanut butter production is encouraging farmers to transfer their output to this crop and so improving the nutritional quality of the diet in the area. Hitherto, their land had concentrated on the production of rice and maize which are the only crops the government guarantees to buy. In March 1989, *Intermediate Technology News* also reported that other areas of assistance are under active consideration including the development of a rotary drum roaster to improve the consistency and volume of roasting, and peelers to replace the hand peeling of nuts.

★ In Malawi groundnuts are widely grown as a cash crop. The oil is an important part of the traditional diet, mainly as a relish with maize meal. A study by the United Nations Children's Fund identified the lack of oils as a contributory cause of nutritional deficiency. One problem is that, until the late Eighties, the producers were only allowed to sell their produce through the national agricultural marketing board. Lever Brothers and other multinationals had a monopoly on both supply and price, so even the farmers who grew the nuts often found it too expensive to buy them back as oil. In early 1989 a project was carried out to make edible oil available at an affordable cost in rural areas.

There are signs that the approach of the Intermediate Technology Group is gaining increasing acceptance. The Prince of

Wales is its patron, and on May 24 1988 the British Minister for Overseas Development visited its headquarters in Rugby, England and came away very impressed with its achievements. Furthermore, since 1986, the organisation has been carrying out the bulk of the technical training of Voluntary Service Overseas, Britain's nearest equivalent to the Peace Corps. So the ideas seem to be spreading and hopefully will get even further acceptance.

ACTION ON POPULATION

In the Introduction, I explained that people in the poor countries wanted more access to birth control. If they obtained it, the birth rate in the underdeveloped countries would fall by a third. Let us consider some more facts.

★ Currently there are 300 million couples in the world who would like to use birth control but do not have it available. Only one third of those in the reproductive age groups have access to family planning.

★ By the year 2000, the global population will be six billion people and there will be 950 million couples of fertile age.

★ The one child family policy in China was introduced partly due to the decline in cultivated land. This, together with the increase in population, led to the amount of effective land per head halving between 1949 and 1989.

★ Population is an important health issue. International Planned Parenthood calculates that with improved birth control we could prevent around 200,000 maternal deaths each year, and that maternal mortality could be halved by the year 2000. In addition, the spacing of births and other family planning related changes, could save the lives of five million infants annually.

★ During their fertile lifetime, women in Latin America are nineteen times as likely to die in childbirth as those in developed countries. Women in South Asia are forty-six times as likely to die in childbirth and those in Africa seventy times as likely to die as women in developed countries.

In the Sixties and Seventies there were two major opposing views of population. Some saw it in apocalyptic terms. One world population report I have from 1978 tells the following story.

A farmer had a big pond, for fish and ducks. On the pond was a tiny lily. The tiny lily was growing. It was doubling in size every day. *"Look" said the people to the farmer "You'd better cut that lily. One* day it'll be so big it'll kill all your fish and ducks".

"All right, all right" said the farmer. "But there's no hurry. It's only growing very slowly." The lily carried on doubling in size every day. "Look", said the farmer several days later, "the lily is still only half the size of the pond. No need to worry yet'. The next day the farmer was very surprised.

This pamphlet stated that if the current growth rate of population had continued since the time of Christ, there would be nine hundred people for every square yard of the Earth's surface and everyone would have to live and work in skyscrapers one mile high.

On the one hand there are those who have been making highly alarming statements and, on the other hand, there are those who do not believe there is any cause for concern. The Catholic Church has been totally opposed to birth control for religious reasons, and some of its activists have attacked the concern with population by pointing out that in some countries density is very low. In Britain and the United States, the anti-abortion organisations publish articles opposing over population worries. It was as a result of the activities of these organisations that led to the United States Government cutting its grant to the International Planned Parenthood Federation in August 1984. It announced that it would cut off its funding to IPPF if *any* funding from *any* sources was used for abortion-related activities. Since the member organisations in the 125 countries were autonomous, there was no way that IPPF could guarantee this. The organisation's press officer, Karen Newman, wrote to me saying that the US withdrawal of support coincided with the most comprehensive agreement ever reached at an international United Nations conference. It led to cuts in staff and, while the strong support from other countries and from private citizens and organisations in the United States has continued, the US action was a body blow for those who have been working to give women the freedom to control the number of children they have.

In recent years, those within the movement for fertility control have been increasingly seeing the issue in the wider context. Barbara Herman of IPPF told me the approach to the problem of population has changed for the better since the 1960's. At this time people were mainly concerned with numbers, *they felt there would be so many people, they would be falling off the end of the world*. She suggested that nowadays there is a far more humanitarian view. Family planning is helpful to parents because it enables them to space their children and look after them much better. In addition, if a woman has eight children, (the average in Kenya) then her health is clearly going to suffer.

A second point is that enabling people to limit the size of their families can result in improvements in the environment. Although population density in some African countries may seem very low, in fact, *137* large areas may be desert and uninhabitable. Furthermore, increasing population may cause more trees to be cut down for firewood with the resultant increase in soil erosion. In 1980 IPPF began publishing *Earthwatch* which considered such related issues as the destruction of forests and wetlands, soil erosion and encroaching deserts. This has helped people realise the interrelationship between population, resources, the environment and development.

In March 1989, the Duke of Edinburgh made some important points in *The Listener*. He drew attention to the fact that the world's population had increased from one billion in 1800. That the second billion took 130 years to add but that the third came in only 30 years. In 1987, the five billion mark was reached, which he said, had important implications for the fixed resources of the earth.

'The wild populations of the seas are being exploited at such a rate that it is becoming only too apparent that it has just about reached the sustainable yield from this source. Any increase in the take from the seas will mean a decline in the breeding stocks and consequently a decline in the exploitable surplus. Exactly this situation arose not many years ago with the herring population in the North Sea. It is now happening on a global scale. The fishing nations of the North Sea were able to agree that all herring fishing should be suspended to allow the population to recover. It took nearly ten years. It is a moot question whether the same could be done for the threatened species of fish on a global scale'.

He continued to say that other people exploit wild animals and birds to augment their diet, but that as the population grows, the habitat of these animals is destroyed and they will decline in number unless precautions are taken. This underlined his interest in the World Wildlife Fund.

Such comments contribute towards the increasing awareness and all is not gloom. There have been successes in some countries in reducing family size. Singapore is probably the best example, with the average number of births per woman dropping from six to two in only just over a quarter of a century. In more dispersed countries such as India, there has also been some progress. However, a great deal remains to be done. One problem is the Catholic Church's opposition to birth control. This has little effect in rich countries like Britain and the United States, however, poor uneducated people are more likely to believe the strictures of the Church. Also the Church Authorities can, in Catholic areas, prevent the setting up of birth control facilities and were responsible for the cut off of US government aid to the world-wide population programmes.

INTERNATIONAL PLANNED PARENTHOOD FEDERATION

This organisation divides the world into six regions which are convenient in order to consider the current position.

- In Africa, the total fertility and infant mortality rates are amongst the highest in the world. Whereas worldwide, about half the world's couples are using modern methods of contraception, in most African countries the figure is less than ten per cent. The family planning services aim to set up an institutional base for satisfying demands for family planning and to promote it as an integral part of health care.

Amongst the most needy countries in terms of assistance are Senegal, Tanzania, Sierra Leone, Ghana, Nigeria and Benin. Nigeria had an estimated population of 112 million in 1988 which is expected to rise to 161 million by the year 2000. Its infant mortality rate of 122 per thousand live births indicated that Nigerian children had fifteen times the chance of dying in the first year of life as those in Norway and Canada. The Planned Parenthood Federation of Nigeria has a number of targets. Some are to reduce the population growth rate from nearly 3% to only 2% by the year 2000, to achieve birth spacing of at least two years for 50% of women and to reduce pregnancies to women under the age of eighteen by 50% by 1995.

Kenya has the highest population growth rate of any country. Its people have traditionally needed many children to help on the farm and for every child that survived it was likely that another would tragically die young. After two decades of improved heath care, Kenyans are now beginning to believe that their children will survive and are adopting family planning. Its Association started beaming its message by radio in 1980 with a programme aiming to tell of the benefits of the small family. It features satisfied family planning users telling their own stories and is very popular.

Intermediate Technology reports that the growth in population, together with the changing patterns of land use and disease, has meant that farmers need new skills and technical improvements. Although population density is still well below that of some countries, less than a fifth of the land is arable. So rapid advances in the spread of birth control methods are needed as part of a general process of development.

- Indian Ocean. This region includes China, India, Hong Kong, Indonesia, Fiji, Australia and New Zealand. Its priorities are sustained information, education and communication activities *139* and to achieve greater government commitment to the population question.

One country with special family planning needs is Bangladesh. In 1988 its population was estimated at 110 million of which 50 million were under the age of fifteen. Less than one in four of the population is literate and its maternal mortality rate is 600 per 100,000 live births. The priorities of the family planning leaders are to encourage community participation in primary health care, to advocate family planning to locally influential groups and religious leaders and to provide information to vulnerable groups such as young men and women.

China has over one billion people and in the years 1980 to 2000, is expected to add over 230 million people to its population — roughly the number of people that live in the United States. The concern about overpopulation led to the one child policy being introduced in 1980. This aimed to limit the population to 1.2 billion by the year 2000 and lower it to 700 million within 75 years. However, it has not been successful and problems arose including the hiding of children and infanticide of baby girls. On the issue of voluntary as opposed to compulsory birth control, it seems clear that the expansion of people's freedom to control their fertility is not only the right thing to do, but is also the most effective.

Dr Qu, one of China's most outspoken environmentalists, has argued that China's growing population will increase the pressure on the environment. There is a need for birth control to keep the increase in population in harmony with the economy and the carrying capacity of the environment. One of China's problems is a shortage of fresh water — it has only one quarter of the world's average. A 1985 survey of its 324 cities found that over half were in water deficit, and in 40 the shortfall was critical. The temptation to use the groundwater has led to its level falling and resulted in subsidence in cities like Beijing and Shanghai. So the restriction of population growth is important to ensure the problem is not exacerbated.

- Arab World. In this region there is a greater demand for services than can be met. So the family planners aim to expand and improve existing services. In some countries the low status of women and the macho nature of the men leads to problems which education needs to combat. However, in recent years there have been some notable changes. The Family Planning Association of Algeria was set up. Relations with the Arab League are about to lead to the family planners being given full membership in the Arab League commissions dealing with health, population, women, youth and social affairs. In addition, Egypt is modernising its clinics, and in 1987 Aden opened its first family planning clinic.

In Morocco there has been a more positive attitude from the political authorities. Since 1977 its Family Planning Association has been taking information to the rural areas. Mobile teams operate with the services of private nurses, midwives, rural stores and Red Crescent centres.

- Western Hemisphere. In this region, countries in need of special assistance include Brazil, Ecuador, Haiti, Mexico, Nicaragua, Honduras and Peru. The family planners have set themselves three major priorities for the years to come. These are the expansion of the quality and quantity of services, the mobilisation of public opinion by forging better contacts with community leaders and building up the organisational strength of the movement.

Colombia shared the United Nations population award in 1988 in recognition of its 23 years work during which the population growth rate has dropped from over 3% to 1.7%. Its infant mortality rates had dropped to 48 per thousand live births which is still much higher than it could be, but is much lower than many comparable countries.

- Europe. In this region, the 22 countries have amongst the highest contraceptive usage in the world. However, there are still many gaps. The abortion rate in many countries would be reduced a great deal if birth control education was improved. An interesting statistic is that in the middle 1980's, for every 1,000 girls reaching the age of eighteen, while only 7 in Holland will have had an abortion, in Britain the number is 20 and in the United States it is 60. So girls under the age of eighteen in the United States are eight times as likely to have an abortion as those in Holland.

Despite the availability of universal education, my research has found great gaps in sex education in Britain and the United States. In *Abortion Practice in Britain and the United States*, I suggested ways that improvements in birth control facilities and education could markedly reduce the abortion rates.

AIDS. One spur to the development of birth control is the concern about the Aids virus. It scared the government in Britain into lifting the ban on condom adverts on television, for example. At the end of February 1988, just over 80,000 cases had been reported from 130 countries. Estimates suggest that between 5 and 10 million people have been infected with the Aids virus and, as its average incubation period is eight years, it is likely to spread a great deal. One way people have tried to contain the disease is to spread such slogans as 'Sex is fun. . .but stay with one'. These injunctions to fidelity may have

141

some limited effect. However, one area that concerns me is that the birth control services have been overwhelmingly female orientated. Research for my earlier book showed that when people began to first have intercourse they more often used male methods than female ones. However, birth control clinics were much more likely to propose female methods. These may be more efficient but give little protection against venereal infections. In all we can see that the issue of population growth is very important and that it needs to be given much greater priority as a way of protecting the quality of people's lives and the environment.

CONCLUSION

This chapter shows clearly that the world as a whole needs to reconsider its goals. The evidence is clear that we will not be able to eliminate poverty unless we move away from high technology solutions and high armament expenditure. We need to give resources back where they belong — with the people — and do what we can to end the current exploitation. If we change our priorities we can place people in a position where they can have the number of children they want, where they can control their own lives and develop an economy which helps the environment rather than damages it.

Chapter 7

WHAT YOU CAN DO

We have seen in the latter part of the 1980's enormous changes in Eastern Europe which have involved important decisions being taken about the future and people being given freedoms not thought possible five years ago. What we now need is for the Western European countries and the United States to make important choices of a different kind. The time has come for rich countries to change their perspective away from the pursuit of ever-increasing wealth and towards improving the quality of life, not only for today's citizens but also for future generations. Currently countries see themselves in competition with each other to develop markets and sell their goods. It does not have to be like that. Instead of constantly worrying about whether their economic growth is better than their neighbour's, or whether their level of inflation is likely to damage their exports, countries should be concerned with their contribution to the major problems facing the world. The kinds of crucial questions that need to be asked are what is Japan's contribution towards protecting the rainforests? What is the United States doing to help with the problem of overpopulation? What is Britain doing to help the solution of food shortages in Africa? What is the Soviet Union doing to protect endangered species of animals? These problems are not usually among the principal concerns of politicians. A change in direction is therefore needed to give higher priority to solving these difficult problems.

Public opinion can play a large part in influencing governments to make the necessary changes. The unprecedented growth in interest in the environment has led to the major parties in the rich countries putting a green tinge on their policies. However, what we need is not *143* window dressing but a revolution in politics. This will come about when the public becomes more aware of the level of damage being caused by governments and the possibilities available for the redirection of resources. It is to encourage such awareness that this book has been written.

The pressure from the current society is to be competitive, to maintain high levels of consumption, acquire the most up-to-date goods and for the individual to climb as high as possible up the ladder of success. In the United States, one of the most commonly used expressions is 'Nice guys finish last'. This idea that it is necessary to be ruthless and aggressive to succeed in life is, however, untrue. The reality is that we need not give in to pressure. We can make our own decision to work towards a society in which people will have the opportunity to flourish, develop their personalities and not have to repress their warmer and more sensitive sides in order to succeed.

By individuals and countries changing their perspectives, we will be able to build a new order. We *can* remove poverty from the world, house people, provide good health care and ensure everyone is adequately fed. The technology is available. We need to change our priorities and values in order to bring these things about.

Let us briefly review the major points from earlier chapters. Chapter One sets out some of the problems facing the world and also areas where improvements have already been made. It also outlines some of the alternative approaches to these problems. It shows that economic theory often predicts that the best way to proceed is for people to pursue their own interests. There are, however, grave limitations to this approach, for it ignores the importance of helping others without seeking any benefit. Richard Titmuss in his book *The Gift Relationship*,showed the value of people altruistically giving blood as a voluntary contribution towards the good of society and he contrasted this to the inferior method of selling it and the fact the blood bought was often contaminated. The value of altruism cannot be measured but is an important aspect of community life. It flourishes in societies which aim to give security to their citizens. People then do not have to spend too much time thinking of their own needs but have time and energy to help others.

Chapter One also sets out the approach of this book which is to move away from the pursuit of ever-increasing wealth and the belief that this will, in some ill-defined way, lead to better social conditions. Instead it maintains we should work directly to improve society. Chapter Two shows the way that wealth and economic growth are very poor indicators of the quality of life. There are many ways that measured wealth can increase without any real benefit to society.

Chapter Three is in some ways a key one. It maintains that in place of the past aims of amassing wealth, we should be pursuing growth in some key areas of production, stability in other sectors and reductions in areas of overproduction. It notes that in some of the most important parts of the economy — food and drink, transport and energy — the crucial factor is the need to work for improvements, with due consideration given to the optimum level of production and consumption. The fourth chapter on health considers ways in which the profit motive in medicine can be more damaging than curative, and that a move to environmentally-friendly policies can help to improve health care. Another important point made in this chapter is that the level of care should be biased towards people's needs and not only on their ability to pay. Chapter Five on crime argues that its high level in developed societies can be directly linked to the over-emphasis on material goods. That if we exercise choice and build the kind of world where money is not considered to be the basis of a good life then crime is likely to diminish. If we develop the kinds of values where people are more interested in what they can contribute to the world, rather than what they can get out of it, then we will have the foundation on which to build a more caring society. If we can teach our children that violence towards others is not a sign of strength but an exhibition of weakness, then we can develop a society where, once again, people will not be scared to walk the streets at night. Overall the chapter shows that the way to reduce crime is not to think in terms of punishing the criminals but rather to work to develop a society that does not produce them in the first place.

Chapter Six on world poverty shows that the traditional growth-related models cannot solve the problem, However, by reducing defence expenditure and turning a proportion of the money over to a more important 'war on poverty' we can make immense improvements. Furthermore, by developing small-scale energy-efficient methods of working, we can have a development aid that is environmentally friendly and will not contribute to the high levels of pollution and global warming. By developing family planning services, we can reduce the number of unwanted children and improve family health and the quality of life.

So we can see there is an alternative path we can choose to take. It will not only benefit us now, but also future generations. The question is what can the average person do to help achieve it? It is to this question we now turn.

WHAT YOU CAN DO

We each have an influence on society and a part to play in producing social change. Throughout the book, I have made suggestions for changes. These can be at the local, national or international levels and now I bring some of those ideas together.

LOCAL CHANGES

It is important for people to consider their lifestyle in relationship to the environment and the quality of life. There are those in high status occupations who command large incomes and yet do great damage by wasting scarce resources, creating tension in society and by their lack of concern about their relationship with the world. In contrast, others protect the environment, conserve resources and work towards a better world. We need to know where we stand on this issue and, if necessary, change our lifestyle. What we contribute to society is much more important than what we receive.

Let us now be a little more specific and make a few suggestions which follow from the logic of this book.

Home There are a number of things we can do in our homes. One is to insulate in order to prevent heat wastage and save energy. Another is to make sure that our heating levels are not excessively high. Many people could save energy by using solar energy. Hundreds of well-insulated solar houses have been built in the harsher climates of north America and Sweden at very little extra cost. For many existing homes, the sun's contribution can be increased by the use of larger windows, solar panels or conservatories on the south side.

Food and Drink We should refuse to buy unhealthy food, or goods in disposable packets and so encourage the market to respond by not producing these things. By buying free-range foods, we encourage the improvement in the conditions for animals. If we eat meat we should ensure it is produced in a cruelty-free way. When we buy fruit and vegetables we should try and ensure that they have not been damaged by the use of pesticides.

By recycling food packaging such as cartons, cans or bottles, we not only help the environment but encourage others to reconsider their position. A group of us began paper recycling at the local school. This took a little time to organise but had many benefits. It had an important educational function for the parents and children as they discussed the reasons for recycling, it is helping reduce the landfills, saving some of the scarce energy resources of the world and also raising money for school funds.

Transport By using energy-efficient methods — trains, buses, cycling and walking instead of cars as often as possible we are helping to finance public transport thus preserving the infrastructure as well as saving energy. By walking we are helping to increase the sociability on the streets and, in so doing, make them safer and more friendly places. By cycling instead of driving we are getting exercise, avoiding polluting the atmosphere and eliminating the risk of accidents and danger to the health of others.

Health and Education By working within the system to improve these services, we help not only ourselves but the local community. There are those who take the view that they will look after their own interests, educate their children privately and use private medicine. However, if this happens on a large-scale, we would develop a society with several tiers all based on wealth. It would work towards the deterioration of life for the poorer groups and this deprivation could result in increased crime. If people stay and work towards improved public services in their own areas then there will be overall improvement for everyone.

NATIONAL

The first point to note is that to a great extent, politicians are not the people who generate change — they respond to it. This can be seen very clearly in the way that in recent years, they have altered their policies in an attempt to woo the voters who are concerned with the environment. The general public have become more aware of the difficult environmental issues facing the world and politicians have had to respond. The important thing is to win the battle of ideas.

Using our power within a democratic society, we should work to get the major parties of all political groupings to make changes in their policies. We need to spread the idea that we need not wait for economic growth to enable us to have a better quality of life. We should be making the necessary changes now.

The view of the world now predominant amongst the major parties is that there is a state of competition between societies. They often take the view that we should be creating an enterprise culture where the rewards are distributed only to those who succeed within this system. However, we have seen how this kind of culture leads to a waste of resources, the disruption of the relationship between parents and their children, an increase in crime and a great deal of tension which leads to alienation and people being unable to fulfill their potential in terms of cultural development. We should encourage the Government to move away from this consumerist view of the world.

Major changes are needed in social policy to give the basis of life to all. The power of the roads lobby needs to be combated. We should promote public transport and recognise the benefits to society as a whole of an integrated transport system which is reliable, safe and clean. Instead of financing large road building programmes, efficient bus, train and underground services should be set up with special con- *147* sideration given to the possible problems of the elderly and children. In addition, late night services should be available for teenagers and others who wish to travel safely after midnight. Particular attention should be given to ensuring that timetables are accurate so that people can plan their trips without wasting time.

In addition, a National Cycling Advisory Council should be set up to promote policies favourable to cycling with national investment available for facilities. In Britain, Friends of the Earth have called for £1,000 million over five years. Such a sum would give the provision of safe cycle tracks a good headstart. A further point is that new developments and road repair schemes should contain plans for cyclists and shops and offices should provide cycle parking. Measures to enforce speed limits for cars will improve road safety. There should be encouragement of smaller cars which are much more energy-efficient as well as antipollution devices such as the catalytic converter.

International We need to promote harmony, co-operation, consideration and a world society in which rich people are concerned with their contribution to the good of humanity. We have seen how few countries contribute help, in even the modest amounts called for by the United Nations. World poverty needs to become the number one priority so that everyone, from whatever country, has proper access to shelter, food, health and education. Furthermore, everyone should be free to speak their mind and not be discriminated against on any grounds such as race, religion, age, sex, class.

We are a long way from this kind of world yet it is a realistic ideal. We do have the potential. All that is needed is to change the goals away from producing wealth and transitory or disposable goods and towards improving society. If we support organisations such as Intermediate Technology or the major charities helping world poverty, we can not only do something to help others but also make a political statement to governments that people do care about each other.

This is of central importance in the reduction of crime. As previously stated once society has changed so that money is of less relative importance because the basics of life are readily available to all, then crime rates will fall. This will be particularly true if we integrate teenagers into society and make use of the idealism of youth rather than as at present, putting half on an academic treadmill and leaving the rest to find their own way in the world. One big problem in recent years is the increase in violent crime. I have already pointed out that changing the sex roles will reduce the number of rapes. Furthermore we need to pay attention to violence on television. One problem is that it is the most violent of the developed societies — the United States — which sells the most programmes around the world. Although the evidence is not conclusive, I feel there is a case for much less violence in television.

A SMALL STEP

Governments have shown a few signs of moving in the right direction. The changes in the Soviet Union have led to a realisation that defence expenditure can be reduced. In the first six months of 1989, the United States cut defence jobs by 13,000 nationally. This is a minute figure bearing in mind that three and a quarter million Americans work in the military industry and related facilities, however, it is one tentative step, in the right direction. Even small reductions in armaments could make a great deal of difference if the money was redirected in the right directions. According to Dr Hiroshi Nakajima, Director General of the World Health Organisation, eleven million children who die every year in the Third World could be saved by the rich countries *for less than the cost of 20 modern military planes*. This fact reinforces the points made in Chapter Six about the excessive militarisation of the world.

Governments are beginning to carry out a few ecologically sound projects which will be well publicised. There is the danger that the public will be hoodwinked into thinking that this well publicised minor tinkering will really change things. It is therefore important to keep in touch with such organisations as Friends of the Earth which is monitoring the British government to see how it performs. In fact all the developed countries need to make major changes and some of these are as follows:

★ The current enormous energy wastage should be reduced. There should be movement towards renewable energy resources. Electrical goods should be labelled with energy consumption figures to improve efficiency. These are the quickest and easiest ways of reducing carbon dioxide's contribution to the greenhouse effect.

★ *Pollution.* The cleanliness of natural water and air should be a priority and laws should be passed to prevent companies from causing pollution. There should be an introduction of the 'precautionary principle'. Companies should have to prove that the discharges are harmless and all dumping of industrial waste into the sea should cease. The public transport system should be greatly improved to reduce the pollution from cars and trucks. This will also reduce the danger to children of accidents. Britain should abolish large tax subsidies to cars which amounted to over £2 billion in 1989.

★ *Population.* By supporting organisations concerned with the problems brought about by increasing population, we can aid people to control their lives and improve their health. Help from governments is particularly important. The British organisation Population *149*

Concern has proposed a number of actions. These include:

★ A programme to extend literacy to all adults by the end of the century.

★ Increased development aid to improve the capacity of the less developed countries to grow their own food and prevent malnutrition.

★ A ten year expansion of family planning programmes to reach an initial 100 million couples.

★ Supplementary feeding to ensure full development for 200 million malnourished children.

★ Supplementary feeding for 60 million malnourished pregnant and lactating women to protect their health and reduce infant mortality.

★ A preventative and community orientated training programme for a sharp increase in the number of medical auxilaries.

★ The development of hygienic drinking water supplies and sewage systems in order to reduce by half the incidence of diseases like typhoid, dysentery and cholera.

These changes would be a modest start in the right direction.

IMPROVING THE ENVIRONMENT

The destruction of topsoil and the rainforests needs to be brought to a halt, and instead a policy of soil improvement instituted so we pass on a rich and fertile world to future generations. We need to work towards the improvement of the oceans and freshwaters to protect rare species and ensure that the variety of life is preserved.

In all we have a great opportunity to change the world, get rid of poverty and develop a new and more healthy international society. The means are available, what is needed is the will to change.

Index